KEL CARPENTER

USA TODAY BESTSELLING AUTHOR

LUCIFER'S DAUGHTER

QUEEN OF THE DAMNED BOOK ONE

Lucifer's Daughter
Kel Carpenter
Published by Kel Carpenter

Edited by Analisa Denny
Cover Art by Fiona Jayde

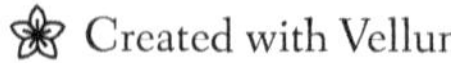

To my tribe, for putting up with me.

"It is true, we shall be monsters, cut off from all the world; but on that account we shall be more attached to one another."

-Mary Shelley, *Frankenstein*

CHAPTER 1

HELL MUST HAVE FROZEN OVER.

That's it. The only possible excuse for why Kendall Clackson, our resident Bible fanatic, was strutting through my favorite diner on a Saturday morning. She usually saved her shenanigans for earlier in the week, on days I didn't have off. Coincidence? Not likely.

I froze in my spot and considered bailing, but that thought only lasted about half a second before her smug face made me stomp across the diner and settle into my usual booth.

Fuck it. I've done the same thing every day for the last ten years. I'm not changing now.

Swinging my legs into the booth, I didn't even pick up the menu as Little Miss Georgia Peach approached me with all her southern charm.

"Ruby! What a pleasure seein' you here, hun."

I turned fractionally and nodded once, hoping she would get the hint. If there was anything that Kendall didn't understand, it was how insufferable I found her exaggerated southern accent to be. We lived in Portland for devil's sake.

"I hope you weren't comin' here lookin' for Josh. He's playin' golf with some of the other men in our church. Bless him. Found his way to the Lord through me."

I could barely contain rolling my eyes. *Oh, yes. I'm sure he did. Just as soon as you gave him what I wouldn't.* I snorted to myself, but didn't say anything. Kendall made it her job to remind me, and everyone else, that he had left me for her and God.

"What's so funny? You know, Ruby, you should find a church. It might help with your"— she dropped her voice low—"*issues.*" Several regulars threw us curious, and somewhat scathing glances. It was an unspoken rule with us Saturday folks that you kept to yourself and didn't start trouble. Like Kendall was currently doing.

"Issues?" I asked, pretending to be mildly surprised by her comment. I knew damn well what she meant. I had a bit of a temper, but in my defense, there's only so much you can do when you're half-demon.

I waved down Martha on the other side of the diner, and she took one look at Blondie before rolling her eyes. Yeah, this wasn't the first time this had happened, but clearly, *I'm* the one with issues.

"You know, your anger—"

"What can I get for you this morning, Ruby?" Martha asked, appearing beside Kendall and seeming not to notice her at all.

"Black coffee and four orders of bacon, please," I said, not bothering to look at the menu.

Martha chuckled under her breath. "I'm not even sure why I ask anymore," she muttered as she walked away.

Kendall resumed her preaching, knowing full well her advice was unwanted. "You know, Ruby, you really should lay off the fat if you ever want to find a nice Christian man."

Something like heat prickled inside me, but I clamped down on it hard. Kendall could pick at me all she wanted. I knew it wasn't actually me she was angry with. It was my cheating ex-boyfriend that wouldn't leave *me* alone, despite my repeated attempts to send him away. It wasn't unreasonable that she was pissed with him. It was unreasonable that she stalked *me* for it, and made *my* life hell. Particularly, when she was the one he had cheated on me with in the first place. Yet, somehow, she didn't see the irony in all of this.

"Hmmmm...let me think about that. Bacon or church? Bacon or church? Well, it's really a no brainer, Kendall. I'm atheist, so I think I better go with the bacon," I said, smirking at the way her mouth popped open. I did enjoy riling her up. What could I say? I have a penchant for trouble.

"Is that Satan talkin,' or just your jealousy, Ruby? You should've known that Josh would find his way to our Lord, with or without you."

This was too much. I couldn't hold back my laughter and I failed miserably when I tried to disguise it as a cough. "Kendall, I hate to be the bearer of bad news, but we split up because he fucked you in a broom closet, and unless 'God' is what you call your vagina nowadays, I think you're fooling yourself." I gave her my most mocking of smiles and made a shooing motion with my hand. Even beneath the orange of her spray tan, I could see her face reddening. She thought she could come here, in my sacred space, and offend me. Slander me and throw my break up out there for everyone to see. She thought it would embarrass me. What she failed to see was that I didn't care. Josh was someone to pass time with, and his dick got the better of him. As a half-succubus, it wasn't my nature to believe in love. Not when the "heart" could be swayed by a pretty face and a three minute fuck.

Kendall's anger seemed to intensify. She put on a saccharine smile as Martha came around the corner carrying my bacon and coffee, but I didn't miss the look in her eyes.

"Bless your heart," she sneered, turning on her heel. I breathed a sigh of relief, but it was a second too early. Her foot came out and caught Martha's black sneaker before I could say anything. Next thing I knew, heat flamed my chest as the coffee splashed across my maroon sweater. It wouldn't burn me, but she didn't know that.

Martha caught herself, but the damage was already done. My bacon lay on the table, soaking in a puddle of coffee that was dripping into my lap.

Her white apron and yellow shirt smeared with grease and coffee, Martha spluttered, "I'm so sorry about that, Ruby! Can I—"

"It's okay, Martha," I said, glaring at Kendall. The bitch had returned to her seat where three other Stepfords sat, each blonde and almost impossible to tell apart. They wore the same impossibly pleasant smiles with their impossibly perfect makeup. Kendall had strength in numbers and gave me a little wave for show as she took her seat.

I. Saw. Red.

Standing from my seat, I hastily helped Martha clean up the mess. She kept repeating to me: "She's not worth it, Ruby." Not that it mattered. Someone needed to teach Ms. Upstanding Citizen a lesson. This was the third time she'd tried to corner me this week, and while it was funny playing with her, what she just did was unacceptable. Not that I deserved any of this, but Martha certainly did not. She wasn't even involved. Kendall could fuck with me all she wanted, but dragging Martha into this and nearly hurting her crossed the line of bullshit I was willing to take. It was time for her to reap the consequences for being a shitty human being.

I placed a ten on the table and left the diner without another word. The door jingled as it swung shut behind me, and I turned my eyes on Kendall's baby blue Mustang.

A fit of glee came over me as my inner demon smiled. I went to my car and grabbed the baseball bat and a lighter I kept in the driver's side door.

Josh should have warned you what happens when you play with fire.

CHAPTER 2

"You broke the windows and set her car on fire. It blew up. How do you deny that when we have twenty-eight—no, I'm sorry—twenty-nine witnesses that saw you?" The officer leaned back in his seat, rolling his eyes. The cops picked me up half an hour after I did it, and dragged me back to their cesspool of a police station. Joe-Schmo and I had been going back and forth for the last fifteen minutes as he attempted to persuade me to admit guilt and pay for Kendall's car. Not fucking happening. At least not without a fight.

"They could be lying." I shrugged, leaning back in my own chair and kicking my feet up on the table. My boots clunked against the metal top as bits of mud and grass fell off. They hadn't even bothered to handcuff me when I was arrested, but I wasn't exactly new to this. Me and Joe were on a first name basis. Practically.

"Get your damn shoes off the table, Morningstar," he scolded. Guess we're on a last name basis today. "This isn't a resort. You're in for a lot of fucking trouble if she decides to press charges." Joe swatted at my feet and I pulled them off the table, leaving dirty streaks across the reflective surface.

"I'm not afraid of Kendall. She got what was coming to her," I huffed, crossing my arms over my chest. Joe let out a sigh of exasperation and scratched his head.

"You're not making my job easy, Ruby," he said.

"Where's the fun in that?" I asked, giving him a wink. The man had a pretty average build for any American man over forty who spent a lot of time at his desk and interrogating low priority criminals. It was the same stereotypical build all the movies portrayed: tucked in shirt with a too small belt, neither hiding the spilling beer gut. With his less than impressive physique, developing widow's peak, and crooked nose from being broken one-time too many—Joe was one hundred percent human. He was also the only officer that didn't spend his entire interrogation undressing me with his eyes.

"We're not supposed to be having fun. You're supposed to admit to your crime and try to settle before she calls her lawyer. Why do you always make this difficult? Huh? What's the point when we both know you'll pay the fine?" A sharp knock at the door interrupted his questioning. The chair scraped the tile as Joe scooted back and got to his feet. I listened intently as the second officer leaned over and told him my bail had been paid, taking his leisure of watching me while I cocked an eyebrow and snorted. His tongue flicked out, licking his bottom lip.

Not a chance, buddy. I smirked to myself as Joe

turned back to me, oblivious to the silent encounter I had with the pervy officer.

"You're in luck. Someone paid your bail," Joe said, giving a sad shake of his head. To his credit, he just doesn't know what to do with me. I was more than most humans could handle. We demons were fickle creatures.

"Looks like Moira did get my message after all," I said. Moira was half-banshee and she happened to be my best friend. She hadn't picked up when I called, but I knew she'd come through before I was in here too long. She always did.

"Uh-huh," Joe said, sticking his tongue in the side of his cheek like he had more to say. The officer who delivered the message pulled the door open for me to cross and exit. His body wasn't huge, but he was stocky, and he purposely gave me no space to step through. Taking a deep breath, I shuffled by, "accidentally" elbowing him in the gut as I went. The putrid stench of alcohol and body odor made me gag.

On the other side of the door, I walked down the hall and signed the release papers. Until Kendall officially pressed charges, there wasn't a lot that could be done. I knew she would. And I would have to pay her, because as fun as this was, I had no intentions of sitting in jail any longer than necessary. I had no regrets, though. The look on Kendall's face when she saw the flames was priceless. Pure fucking gold. Moira was going to love this.

I pushed the door open and waved goodbye to the boys in blue. Outside the air smelled fresh. Crisp. The scent of rain still hung in the air. I stretched languidly, the way a cat does after sitting for far too long. I needed to do something. Burn off the energy that never seemed to leave.

I turned to tell Moira as much, but my friend wasn't the one lounging against the side of the police station. A black-haired devil with smoldering eyes stood where she usually waited. His hair was a color so dark, his skin looked ashen. When his amber eyes flicked to mine, I was suddenly very aware of the coffee stains on my clothes.

Keep it together, Ruby. There was nothing human in his fluid grace as he pulled away from the wall and began stalking toward me. Demon. And not a weak one, by the looks of it.

"Who are you?" I asked, narrowing my eyes.

"I just bailed you out of jail. Is that any way to greet me?" His voice dripped with arrogance. Maybe it was the designer suit he wore, or maybe he was just as powerful as I suspected. Either way, I didn't like the tone in his voice.

"I don't know who you are, so unless you start talking, we're done here." I crossed my arms over my chest and stared him down. His lips fell into an easy smirk. I knew that look. That sarcastic smile meant to belittle and demean a girl, expecting me to feel intimidated.

The words *kiss my ass* were only a breath away.

"My name is Allistair." He took another step forward as he spoke; his voice smooth and melodic, dark and captivating. It was bewitching. It was what an incubus did when pulling in their prey.

"I don't appreciate you trying to persuade me. That's rude, you know." Even as I said it, he cocked his head and took a step closer.

"You sensed that? Here I thought I was being subtle," he purred. Something in me said I should run. Not because I thought he would hurt me, which he would, but because the air tasted like something foreign and heady. His scent clung to me; tendrils of power reaching to pull me closer. He was quite strong, and if he touched me...

I needed to get out of here.

There was a reason I avoided demon men like the plague. Anything and everything this side of the Columbia River were drawn to me by a force I couldn't control. With demon men, it was so much stronger, and they were never the types to just let me run.

Oh, no. They would chase, and even as fast as I was, they would catch up.

"What do you want?" I asked, and to my credit, my voice didn't shake. He looked me up and down and my face heated.

"I need you to come with me, Ruby." The way he said my name made my stomach clench.

"How do you know my name?" I asked, looking towards the street as a car screeched around the corner. Moira's beat up, old Camry hit the curb and came to a jarring stop.

"I'll tell you if you get a drink with me," he said. His eyes flicked to the car and narrowed as I inched towards it.

"I'm good. Thanks, though," I said to the amber-eyed stranger as I got in. Moira didn't say anything as we started to drive away.

I looked in the passenger side mirror to see if the

demon was following, but he wasn't. Allistair, if that was his name, was standing right where I left him, clearly pissed off. He took a step in our direction, and even with a parking lot of distance, it made me shiver. Something told me this wasn't the last I would be seeing of him.

ALLISTAIR

It was like she felt nothing at all.

She certainly gave no indication she knew who I was.

I cursed under my breath and walked towards my car. The sleek, black Audi R8 was the only thing that had brought me joy in the nearly twenty-three years I waited to see her again.

But she didn't remember me.

The thought sent a spike of adrenaline to my system, but the feeling wasn't welcome. All it made me want to do was fuck, or fight. I ran a hand through my hair as I climbed into the car. There was no point waiting around for a girl that wasn't coming back.

I fired up the engine and sat as it purred to life. The steady rhythm usually calmed the instinct to chase a female. Ruby wasn't an ordinary she-demon though, and this wasn't about sex.

I mentally sought out the only one of the three that I thought could do this without fucking it up even more.

"Rysten."

I pulled out of the parking lot and turned onto the highway. I wasn't going back to the penthouse just to report how poorly that went. That I fucked up the one thing I was supposed to be able to do.

"How did it go, mate?"

Anger coiled around my pathetic excuse for a heart.

"Your turn." It was the only answer I could give him as I floored it onto the interstate. My fingers flexed against the steering wheel.

"You want to talk about it?"

I rolled my eyes. He's been spending far too much time with humans if he thought I would want to talk about that.

"Just do your job. I'll be back tomorrow." I weaved through cars as I exited the city, wanting nothing more than to turn around and go back to the girl.

But she had no idea who I was.

Or what she meant to me.

To all of us.

This was the way it was supposed to be, but I don't think any of us were prepared for what we would find when we came for her.

CHAPTER 3

When I arrived at Blue Ruby Ink the next afternoon, Moira gave me a once over and shook her head, dark green hair falling forward. "You must be feeling paranoid," she said.

"Why do you say that?" I placed the two coffees and paper bag on the counter. She continued to stare at my shoulder where Bandit was perched, staring down at the case of belly button rings, rubbing his little paws together.

"You brought the trash panda," she smirked. Bandit jumped onto the glass case, his grabby hands already looking for the fastest way in. I tapped him on the shoulder and wiggled my finger back and forth. He took the hint and wrapped his arms around my neck, hanging there like the big baby he was.

"He's not a trash panda. He's a raccoon," I argued, putting an arm around him. Most people called me crazy for having a raccoon when the majority of pet owners had dogs or cats. Something normal. I didn't want a dog or a cat. I didn't really want any pets until one day I found a baby raccoon following me home from work. He's been with me the two years since—and better trained than most people's children. Apart from the occasional biting problem. But kids do that, too, right?

Moira shrugged and kicked out the barstool next to her. Blue Ruby Ink was the tattoo parlor we'd opened together right after she graduated college at Portland State. I handled tattoos and piercings while she handled all our bills, appointments, and balanced the books.

"So...you want to talk about what happened yesterday?" she asked, flipping through her planner. I settled back onto the barstool next to her and took a sip of my coffee. Strong and black, just the way I liked it.

"Not much to say. Kendall started some shit, so I set her car on fire." Even thinking about it had me smirking. I wasn't sorry I did it, even if I had to pay for a new car. She's had it coming for the last month or so, and it felt damn good to repay some of the hate.

"Not that. The guy in the parking lot."

I gave her a sideways look, but she kept her eyes on the planner. "Just some guy who paid my bail and wanted to take me out for a drink."

"The hell? Just some *guy* that *paid* your bail? What'd you say?" she prodded. Subtle, she was not.

"No, of course." I opened the paper bag and took a huge bite of my double chocolate chip muffin. Calorie counting was for suckers. You only live one life, may as well eat your way through it—least that was my take on it.

"Still staying away from men?"

"Can you blame me?"

She frowned at her planner. "No, but I worry about

what will happen to you," she murmured. I opened my mouth to dispute that, right as the front door chimed.

"How can we help you?" she asked, still not looking up. Too bad for her because there was quite a bit to see.

"I have a consultation with Ruby," he said. I was pretty sure I was staring at a blonde Adonis because there was no possible way his face could be any more handsome. His full lips quirked up at me and I scrambled to stop my staring.

"Name?" Moira asked, flipping back and forth in her planner. I bit at the corner of my thumbnail and ran my hand along Bandit's fur in a nervous gesture.

"Rysten."

"I don't have a Rysten listed," she said, only then taking the time to look up. He would only see her glamor, beautifully neutral cedar skin that masked her true mint green color. I could see through it, watching her cheeks as they tinged pistachio: the tell-tale signs of a banshee's blush, but she didn't seem affected by his presence otherwise. Unlike me. My traitorous pasty white cheeks that turned red under the barest hint of sun, or in this case, blush.

"I'm certain I booked one. Can you check again?" he asked. His eyes never left me, and while he seemed polite and good-natured enough...so was the demon outside the police station.

Moira switched from her planner to the desktop, pulling up my schedule. In the top right corner, first appointment of the day, it said *Rysten*. She stared at the computer silently, blinking three times.

"That wasn't there yesterday," she said matter-o-factly.

"I can assure you that I booked in advance," he said. He sounded amused. With what, I didn't know.

"How far in advance?" she pressed. I sighed, getting up from my barstool to swing open the gate and escort him back to my office.

"Several months. I'll only be in town a short time," he continued, either not noticing her narrowed eyes and twitchy pen, or simply not caring. Moira took her schedules very seriously. She could be nonchalant about picking me up from jail or setting cars on fire, but fuck with her schedule and you'll be dealing with a screaming banshee. I was not willing to sacrifice my eardrums.

"Moira, it's fine. I can take him back and do a consultation. It will only be fifteen minutes," I said, trying to ease the tension. She hissed under her breath.

"It's not about the consultation." Turning to him, she snapped, "What brings you here when you won't be in town long?" I put my palm to my forehead and ran it down my face, sighing in my frustration. I wouldn't say that she's ordinarily sweet to people, because she definitely had some crazy in her, but she wasn't usually this aggressive. When she sniffed trouble, she was a demon through and through.

Rysten took one look at her and smiled, like she was a hissing kitten and not someone that could burst his eardrums in seconds. "I'm here for Ruby," he said, turning his dark emerald eyes on me. The intensity was startling. I took a step back. "Your tattoos are all the rage where I'm from. I knew I needed to check them out for myself," he amended, giving me a boyish grin.

"Right," I drawled out. The awkward silence hung for a moment before I motioned for him to follow me back. Moira opened her mouth to object, but I beat her to the punch. "It's fifteen minutes. Please, just let it go. I could use the extra cash to pay for Kendall's car."

She glared at me and crossed her arms. "Fine. If you're late for your next client, it's on you." I conceded with a nod and closed my office door behind me.

Alone with Rysten, I settled behind my desk and leaned back in my chair, crossing my hands in a steeple under my chin. "So, is this the part where you tell me why I have a demon in my office, asking for a tattoo you don't actually want?"

Across from me, Rysten blinked, his eyes sharpening. The glamor surrounding him pulsed for a moment, but settled back to its nearly undetectable state. He was good; I'll give him that. Nearly as good as Moira was at hiding her green skin. His body had the slightest sheen over it; not a physical glamor. A psychic one.

"Clever girl. What gave me away?" he asked, that lazy smile reappeared like it never left his face. He may look like he just walked off a beach, but that carefree façade wouldn't fool me. Demons were not easy-going creatures by nature. The fact that he glamored himself meant he had something to hide.

I quirked my lips up in a neutral smile. "I can't reveal all my cards, can I? I still don't know why you're here." I wasn't weak, but I was nothing exceptional. I'd yet to come into my powers, if I ever would, and without any real gifts to speak of, it tended to make other, stronger demons view you as prey. It didn't help that the only true power I had was the fact that anything and everything with a dick wanted me. Whether I wanted them or not. Best not to piss anyone off too much until I knew what I was dealing with.

"I already told you why I was here, love," he said kindly. I frowned and scratched behind Bandit's ears to busy my hands. "I'm here for you."

"I'd gathered that much. What I don't know is *why*."

"I'm afraid I can't tell you that just yet," Rysten replied apologetically. "I wanted to get to know you first. Before the others got involved." He rolled his eyes in a very human gesture of annoyance.

"Others?"

"I can't explain that either. They wish to do it together," he answered, shrugging off my attitude. He was infuriating. Yet another reason to stay away.

"Wait...does this have anything to do with the creeper waiting outside the police station last night?" I probably could have been less demanding about it, but it was too strange not to overlook the possibility.

Rysten snorted. "Allistair?" I nodded once. "I look forward to relaying that message to him." Damn it. They knew each other. This was not coincidence, but I didn't get the feeling it had anything to do with them looking to dominate me. Our kind were not subtle in their endeavors, and if that's what they wanted, I think this conversation would be going very differently.

Bandit purred against my chest, clutching me tighter. I glanced down to see his tail was swaying side to side. He was either happy...or agitated. I was hoping happy because dealing with a biting raccoon was not high on the list of shit I felt like dealing with today.

Rysten eyed him, wrinkling his nose, he said, "I have to ask. Why do you have a raccoon?"

I pursed my lips at the mild disgust in his voice. "Why does anyone have a pet?" I asked. It was rhetorical, but he cocked his head like he was seriously considering my question.

"I suppose companionship. It's the only real reason I could see anyone taking in a wild animal." It was both a thoughtful, and yet, a very typical demon outlook. We had the capacity to understand, but not to empathize with most things. My bond with Bandit was abnormal, but I just chalked it up to the half-human in me and left it at that. "He seems quite fond of you," Rysten noted.

"He is."

We locked eyes, a world of silent questions swimming before us. I really wanted to know what the hell he was doing here, but he seemed to be content just watching me and evading my question. "You're not what I expected," he said eventually. I tilted my head, raising an eyebrow. Before I could ask, there was a knock on my door.

"Your first client is here," Moira called. I tapped Bandit's shoulder signaling for him to jump down. He scurried across the floor and up the massive cat tower I kept in my office for when I brought him to work. Most people weren't too fond of raccoons, and he wasn't too fond of most people.

Rysten stood, and I walked around the desk to open the door. My hand stilled on the door knob as I faced him. I was prepared to ask him once again why he was here, maybe even add a little persuasion to the mix in hopes of getting a real answer, but something in his eyes had me frozen to the spot. My mouth went dry at the intensity I found: so very similar to the demon from last night, and yet different. Allistair had a roughness, and an air of danger that edged that dominance. I had no doubts that there was more to the incubus than the cold arrogance he exuded.

Rysten had a different feel. His power was offset with curiosity, like I was the enigma he couldn't figure out. His glamor was still in place; he'd yet to drop it once. There was a flux of something behind it; almost like a ripple of power that he was struggling to contain.

What kind of demon are you?

He reached forward, his fingers only inches from my face, and a knock at the door brought the moment to an abrupt halt.

His hand dropped to his side, a boyish smile lighting his face again as the tension dissipated. I opened the door and stepped through.

"I'll see you again soon, Ruby," he murmured. I turned around to say goodbye, but he was already gone. His words hung in the air, a promise that had my skin heating with anticipation.

I was so royally fucked, and I didn't even know why.

RYSTEN

I don't know what I was expecting after Allistair passed the torch to me, but she wasn't it.

She was warier than I thought she'd be. Cynical. Sarcastic.

I could see why his nature would rub her the wrong way.

She was fiercely independent, that much was clear. She wasn't going to like being told what to do, and given that she had no idea who we were, this wasn't going to go as planned.

The girl I just met was not going to drop everything and come with us. She had a life; albeit an odd one given that she kept vermin as a pet.

Not to mention the receptionist.

The banshee was suspicious. She knew I hadn't booked that appointment. That was going to be problematic. I hooked a left on the corner and stopped inside the first coffee shop I found. Ordering a medium roast with two sugars, I then took a seat by the window and mentally reached out to Julian.

"We need to talk." He was not going to like this, but what were we going to do? Forcibly remove her? No. This needed to be handled with tact; something my brother didn't have.

"I'm meeting with Allistair. What is it?" he replied. I sincerely hoped Allistair had told him how the original meeting went down, or he might try to throttle me.

"I've met with Ruby. We need to have a dis—"

"What do you mean 'you've met with her'?"

Well. That answered that. Pouting fucker hadn't thought to notify him when things went south. *"Speak with Allistair. Come find me when you are done. I'm changing the plan."* I could sense a brief surge of anger before his mind pulled away.

I sipped at my coffee, savoring the bitter burn.

We had her. She was right here.

Except the moment she looked at me and called me on my glamor, I knew we were in trouble.

There was spark of the devil behind her eyes and she doesn't even realize it.

CHAPTER 4

The afternoon passed in a blur as I thought about Rysten's parting words: *soon.* That could mean a lot of things, and I was pretty sure our next encounter would not be alone. He mentioned that there were...*others*. Including the one I already met. The thought sent shivers running down my spine.

"Moira!" I called, and she poked her head around my office door. "My schedule is clear, yeah? I'm going to leave for the night. Feeling a little under the weather." It wasn't a complete lie. I really was feeling strange, just not of the sickly variety.

Moira narrowed her seafoam green eyes. "Wouldn't have anything to do with that guy from this morning, would it?" she asked.

Nosy banshee.

"Why would it have anything to do with him?" I asked, as good a non-answer as I could get. I didn't like lying to her, but I was in no position to handle an interrogation right now.

"You've been acting weird since he left."

Weird. That was one way to put it. I was freaked the fuck out. I had no idea what was going on, but I didn't want to bring it up to her. It was one thing for me to worry when Rysten, and probably Allistair, would show back up for devil knows what. It was an entirely different thing to be calming Moira in that process. She was possessive. She'd hunt them down if she thought they meant to do me harm.

No. Until I knew what they wanted, I wasn't involving her.

I lifted the corners of my mouth in a tired smile and went to retrieve Bandit from his hidey-hole in the cat tower. He practically sprang at me, locking his arms around my neck like a sloth in a tree. "Bandit's been feeling a bit antsy today. I thought getting him out of the house would help, but it's not." I shrugged and turned for the door, hoping that was enough to satisfy her. As far as non-lie-lies go, it was golden. Moira's eyes flicked to him and softened, just a little. Inwardly, I snickered. She could call him a trash panda all she wanted, but I knew the truth. He'd grown on her.

"Get him a can of sardines. He'll be fine," she said indifferently. Bandit started chittering at the mention of his favorite little fish. Damned raccoon. Food was always the number one priority. Now he'd be yapping in my ear the whole way home.

I grabbed my purse off the desk and headed out. "I'll see you at home. Don't forget to lock up." She shooed us out with a hard look and wave of her pen.

Outside, the cool October air hit me full force, my

teeth chattering as my breath fogged white. Bandit curled tighter around me, swinging his tail around my neck like a scarf. Crossing my arms to keep warm, I clutched my purse tighter as I cut down the alleyway that led to the parking lot. The ominous Cimmerian skies were heavy with rain waiting to fall. I trudged on through the grey bleakness, jumping when a large rat scurried past me and into the sewer drain.

My breath came in hot, heavy bursts as I stopped. Paranoia was eating at the edge of my already frazzled mind. I took a hazard glance behind me, just to soothe my beating heart.

Click.

The wrong end of Glock 19 pressed against my forehead.

"Gimme your purse," he said. My attacker couldn't have been older than twenty. The hoodie he wore wasn't inconspicuous in the slightest. Black and white skulls covered the damn thing like they were meant to inflict fear, but how could anyone be afraid when he wore his nose ring like a cow? I couldn't stop the giggle that escaped my lips.

"You laughin'? What you laughin' at, bitch?" He waved his other hand around in some kind of gang symbol and it looked suspiciously like the sign for 'off the hook'. I couldn't even pretend it wasn't ridiculous if my life depended on it. Clearly.

"Hey! I said why the fuck you laughin'?" He raised his voice, moving the gun like he was going to slam the butt of it into my head.

Bandit didn't take kindly to most people, and he sure

as hell didn't tolerate wannabe thugs attacking me. In the time it took to cock his hand back, my raccoon flung at him, landing on his face with his claws out and teeth snapping.

I grabbed the wrist of his hand that was holding the gun. No way was I going to let him start firing that thing blindly. He screamed while Bandit bit down on his nose.

"Motherfucker!" he cried.

Yeah, kid, you're a mother fucking idiot. I slammed my knee into his groin. As I stepped to the side, he fell forward, his hand losing its grip on the gun, dropping it to the ground.

"That's enough," I said to Bandit. Even hissing and spitting, he listened to me, detaching himself from the kid's face. With considerable force, I brought my elbow down on the base of his skull. He let out a muffled cry and collapsed on the ground, unconscious.

I squatted down and picked up the gun. Hopefully, that taught the kid a lesson in trying to rob people, but just in case, I was confiscating the weapon. He didn't need to be running around killing people in alleyways. If I was an unforgiving demon, he wouldn't be leaving this encounter alive.

I reached over and turned his head to the side. The punk had some pretty gnarly scratches that would need stitches, and his entire nose was gone. I glanced over at Bandit. Next to him lay the boy's chunk of nose, with the cow ring still in it.

Ouch. With one hand, I dug my phone out of my pocket and dialed 911.

"Operator. What's your emergency?" I rattled off the

street location and left it at that. The cops would find him soon enough and take him to a hospital to get his nose reattached. I didn't want to feel any guilt over his injuries. I mean, he was going to rob me. I seriously doubt he would have killed me, but you never know.

I sighed, letting go of the blame as I turned to Bandit. His teeth were bared, still hissing at the unconscious boy. He didn't even notice me until I shuffled a foot or two closer, both hands held out, palms open.

"Come here, boy," I murmured. I made little *shh* sounds until he calmed enough to run up my arm and perch himself on my shoulder. The pricks of his claws stung a bit, but I ignored it as I rose to my feet.

I gathered my purse and stored the gun in my waistband, ready to go home and see this day to an end. As I turned to leave the alleyway, I saw that Rysten had made good on his promise. With him was Allistair and another male demon that radiated immense power, even from several yards away.

Shit.

"Hey, there..." I said awkwardly, trying to figure out how to go for the gun without being obvious. Unlike the kid that attacked me, I was smart enough to know when I was overpowered.

They started walking towards me and I panicked, grabbing for the gun.

I held it up, aiming at the three of them, not realizing how much space they'd crossed while I was pulling it out. Only three feet away from the barrel, they surrounded me in a semi-circle.

"Don't come any closer!" I said. My hands visibly shook, making the barrel wobble about unsteadily.

"We're not here to hurt you, Ruby," Rysten said. He held up his hands in a show of surrender, but I wasn't a fool. Any demon worth their salt didn't need their hands.

"Who are you and why the fuck are you following me?" I demanded, swinging the gun towards Allistair as he took a step closer. He looked much the same as yesterday, with his tailored suit and styled hair. But his eyes... he looked pissed from the moment I saw him. *Great. I'm going to be incubus dinner.*

"Ruby, it's time to calm down," Allistair said. His eyes glowed amber and a sudden ease spread through me. I lowered the head of the gun slowly, until it was pointed at his knee instead of between his eyes. "That's right, just calm down. It's all going to be alright." The drowsiness intensified, and it was only Bandit's hissing that brought back a modicum of clarity.

"Stop trying to persuade me, demon, or I will blow your fucking knee cap out," I threatened, knowing full well he could probably kill me before that ever came to pass.

"Allistair, back up. You're making her nervous," the third one said. I turned my eyes on him, only to be struck by the similarities he and Rysten shared. His hair was the lightest shade of blonde I'd ever seen; so blonde it could pass for white. They had the same dark green eyes and light skin, but where Rysten had this hot-boy-next-door thing, this guy had an edge of beauty that was intense. His cheek bones were sharper. His teeth, whiter. His skin didn't have a single imperfection, and the power that rolled off him was not something that wanted to be contained. Couldn't be contained. That insight was all it took for the barrel of the gun to go from Allistair to the unknown guy in front of me. Panic surged at the swell of power that threatened to consume me, making the air hard to breathe. Bandit trembled against my shoulder. His fear consumed me, feeding into my own.

Without realizing it, I pulled the trigger, shooting him right between the eyes.

He didn't even bat an eyelash as it popped right out of his head and clanged against the asphalt. The gun slipped from my fingers and I choked out the only words I could manage to process.

"Who are you?"

"The world knows me as Death, but you can call me Julian."

Holy. Shit. Devil have me, because I think my brain just short-circuited.

"Is this the part where you kill me?" I blurted. I couldn't stop the word vomit that came after. "Because if you do, please don't hurt Bandit. He's a good raccoon, really. My friend Moira says she doesn't like him, but she really does, and she would take care of him and everything—"

"We're not here to kill you, Ruby," Rysten said.

"What?" I asked, looking between the three faces. My eyes landed on the one I'd shot. *Julian.*

"We're here to protect you, Ruby, and right now, that means we need to get out of here," he said.

"So you can kidnap me," I stated bluntly. Allistair growled under his breath, making me jump back. Julian pinched the bridge of his nose and sighed. Sirens blared in the distance.

"No, because you called the police to help the worthless human," Julian said. I blinked, only then registering where he was going. "You don't want to be found here with your raccoon that tore his nose off, his gun in your hands, and him unconscious," he continued slowly, as though he was giving instructions to a child.

"Right," I drawled. I picked up the gun, flicked the safety on, and tucked it in my waistband. Rysten bent down and retrieved the bullet, putting it in his pocket.

"You okay, love?" he asked. I glared up at him, crossing my arms over my chest.

"Cut it out, Rysten. We need to get her home," Julian said. I turned my incredulity on him.

Take me home?

"I can take myself home just fine," I said stiffly.

"No."

No? Who the hell did he think he was?

I opened my mouth to argue and he stepped forward into my bubble of ill-conceived safety. Standing close to that cold persona, that raw power staring down at me, every word I had just dried up.

"You have two choices: I can either throw you over my shoulder and carry you to your home, or we can drive there. Your decision," he said.

Was he joking? No. Definitely not joking.

"Drive," I ground out. I think the ghost of a smirk crossed his lips as we left the alleyway.

JULIAN

She shot me.

And then she begged for the life of a raccoon.

I didn't know whether I should be amused or frustrated. Rysten wasn't wrong. She was not what I expected. We hid her for almost twenty-three years. From everyone. Including ourselves. It would be foolish to think that we know her, or even understand her, after we left her on earth with the humans.

Not a day went by that I did not look forward to finally coming for her.

But I didn't expect to mourn the loss of time.

We had only seen her briefly. She was only a babe, not even an hour old, before her mother took her. Now...

I couldn't deny it. She was all grown up.

I adjusted the rearview mirror in her direction and those brilliant blue eyes met mine. The center was so light, nearly white, but they fanned out into cobalt flames before fading to black. I don't know how she stayed hidden for so long when the dark look in her eyes screamed of trouble.

Ruby was not a little girl, and we'd never known her as one. She was a grown woman. No. She was a grown she-demon who had yet to go through the transition. That made her vulnerable. She could stare at me with bedroom eyes all she wanted. It was our divine duty to protect her. To guard her.

The others may get distracted, but I wouldn't.

Even if a single look from her had me hard.

CHAPTER 5

The heavy silence while I sat in the back of my own car was crushing me. Julian had insisted on driving. With one look, he made me hand over the keys to my 1995 VW bug...and then moved the seat for me to get in the back. It was probably for the best, given that Bandit was riding on my lap, but I wasn't going to tell them that.

At least they gave me a choice about who rode in the back with me. Not that it really saved me. Rysten was just as massive as the other two and had his thigh flush against mine. As if that wasn't enough to make me uncomfortable, he also hadn't taken his eyes off me. Julian had purposefully moved the rearview mirror to face me instead of the back window, and I felt his gaze on me as well. Maybe he just didn't have any kind of self preservation like I did, given that a bullet to the head couldn't make him blink. If I wasn't blushing before, I definitely was now.

I couldn't believe that I shot him. And that he let me live.

"Are you going to tell me who the hell you people are?" I finally asked. Bandit's frustration was leaking through, and I was on edge. He didn't like all the strangers in the car with us anymore than I did.

"Soon." Julian said. "We'll explain it when we get to your house. Laran is almost there already."

"Wait, who's Laran?"

I probably should have been more freaked out that they knew where I lived, but given that Allistair got me out of jail before Moira could arrive, it really wasn't that surprising.

"Another Ho—" Rysten began, until Julian glared at him. "You'll meet him soon enough. He's a friend."

Great. Another one. Well then. I guess that's all there was to it.

Settling back into my seat, I held Bandit closer, stroking his fur to ease him. Blood smudged my clothes where he rubbed his face and paws. I was happy it wasn't his, but I didn't want to think about where it had come from. I lived fifteen minutes from the parlor and it felt like it took twice the time to get there. When we pulled into my driveway, whatever shock I felt faded away at the sight of my sleazy ex-boyfriend.

The car rolled to a stop, but no one in my company made a move to get out. Julian and Allistair shared a look in front of me, like they were seriously considering keeping me in here. Uh...not happening.

Not at all surprising, Josh had the nerve to walk up and tap on the window. Allistair didn't respond. Instead,

Rysten, the one I thought was the most easy-going of the three, said, "We should get rid of him."

"If you let me out, I will deal with it," I said. While the thought of 'getting rid of him' appealed to me as much as setting Kendall's car on fire, I was already in enough trouble with the police.

They shared another look, but it was only when Julian shrugged that both he and Allistair actually got out of the damn car. Allistair silently held the seat forward for me. It would've been a kind gesture, but he barely gave me room. Forced to graze his suit as I squeezed by, my libido went into fucking overdrive. Didn't even touch his skin. His *suit.* The scent of him filled my nostrils, sending tingles...

I was breathing heavy by the time I was standing on my own two feet outside the car, and it had nothing to do with physical exertion. I glared at him, an arrogant smirk on his face.

"Hi, Ruby," Josh said, pulling my attention away. I turned my eyes to him and what I saw was disappointing.

When I met him, he had this whole lost soul thing going on. He kept his hair long and was in a band. I never loved him, but he was a good person to pass the time with. Until Kendall got her claws into him. Looking at him now, it was like two different people. This Josh dressed in Polos and loafers. His hair was short and gelled back, and from five feet away, the cologne he wore was enough to make me want to gag.

"What do you want?" I asked. I could hear the fatigue in my voice. Truth be told, I was fucking exhausted after the adrenaline high I'd already had today. I didn't have the energy to waste on him.

"I wanted to talk..." he started slowly, giving a pointed look at the three guys who stood behind me. I didn't even need to look. There was tension radiating through the air. I could feel it.

"I have nothing to say to you." Bandit growled at him from his perch on my shoulder. Josh paled, but he didn't back away. I sighed. *Idiot boy.*

"That can't be true, Ruby. You blew up my girlfriend's car. I know you still care," Josh said, even going so far as to take a step towards me. I didn't want to step back, because it looked weak. But I was worried Bandit might actually attack him. He'd never liked Josh, and right now he was being very protective of me and wanted him gone.

"That's because your girlfriend's a bitch. Don't confuse the facts," I said dryly. Without warning or permission, a strong arm wrapped around my waist. I tensed, worried that my raccoon's anger was going to turn on the person who had just touched me, but it appeared that Bandit was dead set on wanting to get rid of Josh, and only Josh.

"Is this"— he stammered—"Is *this* why you won't return my calls?" He motioned to the beautiful trio of men, his eyes bulging out. I could see what was coming next. "You wouldn't even have sex with *me*, and you have—"

My eyes flashed. "I'm not answering your calls because you and I are no longer dating. We are not a thing. We aren't even friends. What I do now is none of your concern." I had to work to keep the growl out of my voice.

Yeah, I didn't have sex with him. I didn't have sex with anyone because it was never a conscious choice. I could pick any guy off the street and he would fuck me then and there if I wanted, thanks to dear old Mom. So, despite my nature, I didn't fuck anyone. And this was what I got for it.

The boy actually had the nerve to take another step towards me. "This isn't you, Ruby. I remember. I know you. You wouldn't be with these"—he broke off, searching for a word that would suffice to describe the three stunning demons that were unlike anything this earth could produce. Even in his sub-conscious human mind, something registered that they were more than men—"*people*." Someone snorted behind me, and I was pretty sure which one, given that only one of them had a sense of humor from what I could tell. The laughing stopped short when Josh said, "Come back to me."

"Why on earth would you think I am ever coming back to you?" I scoffed. I probably would have laughed had the arm around my waist not tightened slightly as he let out the tiniest of growls. It was so low I almost didn't hear it, but it was there. I looked up to see Julian.

My heart skipped a beat as I swallowed hard. My throat was dry and scratchy, but there was something so protective and feral about the way he looked at Josh that just made a girl wonder what a little taste of that might be like. To have a demon like Julian's complete and utter attention...

Pure bliss? Or pure hell?

Somehow, I thought he might be a bit of both. They say pain is pleasure, if you know what you're doing.

Damnit, Ruby. You need to focus. Now isn't the time to be thinking like a sex-deprived maniac.

Josh cleared his throat, and I blinked. *Shit. Did he say something?* I glanced back at my stuffy ex with his posh ironed khakis.

"I made a mistake, Ruby. I'm sorry—"

"I gotta stop you right there. We both know you're going to go home after this, screw Kendall, and then come back another day to 'beg' for my forgiveness. So, can we just skip all the unnecessary bullshit, and move on like adults? Because I'm really getting tired of her taking out her issues with you"—I pointed a finger at his weak chest —"on me."

I had really hoped it would work this time. That being straight-forward would do the trick. Silly me, thinking that Josh could think with his brain and not his dick. He didn't consider the words for more than four seconds before inserting his foot in in his mouth. Again.

"Ruby. Please. Let's just talk this out. I miss you," he whined. *Damnit. Not the whining.*

My patience was already running thin and he just stomped on the last layer that was positioned between him and the brutally frigid truth that came pouring from my lips.

"Go home and lay in the fucking bed you made. You cheated on me. I'm not coming back to you, and this is your last warning. Move on." The pissed off look in his eye would have been funny, but I knew he'd forget about it soon enough. Then he'd be right back here on my doorstep, begging for something he'll never have.

"I think it's in your best interest that you leave now, while you still can." The menace in this voice sent chills down my spine. I turned to the figure that came strolling up my driveway.

Holy. Hell. His hair was so dark, it looked black...but when the light from the streetlamps hit it, I saw flashes of pure, undiluted *red.* He was the tallest of the four, with fierce black eyes and a savageness about him that told people he was not one to be fucked with.

Josh took a single look at him and I thought he was going to piss himself. While they still scared the shit out of me, I'd shot one and they still haven't killed me. That's a pretty good reason to think they won't. Josh didn't have that courtesy, and if he continued to stay here running his mouth about our lack of a sex life, I might decide to say 'fuck it' and let Bandit at him.

"Don't make me call the police, Josh," I said, knowing it wouldn't get that far. He was an idiot and a cheater, but he didn't want trouble with the law.

After one particularly snobbish look around, he got in his car and drove off.

I couldn't contain the sigh of relief as his tires squealed around the corner of my street, but that relief was short-lived. Only then did I realize Julian's arm was still around my waist. I was becoming increasingly aware that I may have just traded one bad situation for another.

They haven't killed you yet, I reminded myself. May as well get it over with. I stepped away from Julian, putting space between me and the four demons that sucked the air from my lungs.

"So, is this where you finally tell me who you are and why you're following me?" They didn't look at each other, but each of their faces was set in grim determination.

"I am Pestilence," Rysten said.

No...

"I am Famine," Allistair followed.

Devil save me.

"I am Death," Julian continued in a cool tone.

It should have clicked with me sooner.

"My name is Laran, and I am War," the fourth and final one said.

They didn't continue because they didn't need to. I knew who they were. Every demon in both worlds knew who they were.

"You're the Four Horsemen," I whispered.

CHAPTER 6

I WAS HAVING A HARD TIME WRAPPING MY HEAD around the identity of the strangers sitting in my living room. Even with a hot cup of tea and ten minutes to digest, there were some things that life simply can't prepare you for. The Horsemen were one of those things.

They were four of the most powerful arch demons ever created, only usurped by one power and one power alone: the devil himself. Which begged the question: why were all four of his personal guard stalking me and not back in Hell where they belonged?

"So..." I started in a slow, weary voice, "did I do something? This isn't about Kendall's car, right? I mean, I feel like you would have mentioned it by now, but—"

"This isn't about the car," Allistair said. He watched me like a cat did a mouse. The feeling was unnerving, but it also made my stomach clench in all the ways that were not helpful right now. With his ankle propped on his knee and hand stretched over the back of the couch, I couldn't tell if the small space he'd left between himself and Rysten was an invitation or pure coincidence. I averted my eyes to look away, but found myself staring at Julian instead.

"We need you to come back to Hell with us," Julian said.

"Wait, what? No! Why?" I asked, skimming the others. He was kidding, right? He had to be joking. A half-breed like me wouldn't survive in Hell. I'd be turned into some other stronger demon's plaything, and that's if I was lucky. My eyes landed on Rysten as I began shaking my head no. "Why?" I repeated, when no one gave me an answer.

"Because you're Lucifer's daughter," Laran said. Rysten cringed, but didn't deny it.

Allistair rolled his eyes. "Way to go, War. Why not just drop it on her even though we agreed—" I burst out laughing.

I laughed—no, I roared—so hard I was tearing up in the corners of my eyes. They thought—what? They thought *I* was Lucifer's *daughter*? Oh, this was rich! Beyond rich. I laughed while they stared at me in stunned silence. Oh-ho-ho, they were here because they thought I was important! They didn't kill me because they thought I was the devil's daughter. Well, the joke's on them! I'm just a half-breed succubus with an affinity for picking up trouble.

"Ruby..." Rysten trailed off. "Why are you laughing?"

"You think"— I cracked up again—"you think I'm the *devil's daughter*."

"You are," he frowned.

"No, Rysten. I'm half-human," I said kindly. I don't

know who told the Horsemen I was the King of Hell's daughter, but whoever it was better be running. I doubted they would be pleased when they found out the truth.

"Who told you that?" Julian asked.

"The demon orphanage I grew up in. My mother dropped me off in Atlanta hours after I was born. Told them she wouldn't have a half-human baby, and that was that," I shrugged. The story was slightly uncomfortable for me, but I'd grown to accept it. Demons were either obsessive or apathetic; there wasn't a lot of in-between. If my birth mother thought I was a waste of genetic material, then that was her problem. It wasn't my fault she screwed a human and got pregnant. That's why there were orphanages in the first place. For the unlucky offspring of demons that wanted nothing to do with their mistakes, but someone still had to teach us how to glamor ourselves from the humans. Hell forbid the rumors of our kind ever become more than just that. Then again, if Hell really gave a damn, they'd close the portals between the worlds and be done with it.

"Your mother. Was her name Lola Morningstar?" Julian asked. I nearly choked on my sip of tea and narrowed my gaze in his direction.

"You probably pulled that off my birth certificate," I said coolly.

"Or I knew her," he responded in jest. A hard, icy tone had entered his voice making me shiver.

"Right," I drawled. I didn't believe that story.

"She brought you here to hide you," he argued.

"Because I was Lucifer's child?" I asked. Snickered, really. Julian didn't seem to find it very funny.

"Yes, and some very powerful demons wanted to kill you for it. They still do," Laran interjected.

They truly believed this nonsense. That I was some miracle baby.

Lucifer has been around longer than any of us, and as far as anybody knows, he doesn't have any children. Some rumors say he can't. Others say he doesn't want to share his power. Either way, in the thousands of years he's been on this earth and in Hell, not once has anyone come forward saying they have his child.

I was not going to be the exception.

"Let's say that you're right. *I* am Satan's spawn. Lola hid me to keep me away from all the people I'm assuming have a bone to pick with him?" I paused, they nodded. "So, answer me this: even if I was, why do I need to go to Hell? Aren't I better off living my life here where no one knows I exist?"

They all seemed to share a glance.

"Have you ever heard the story of the Four Horsemen?" Laran asked.

"Of course. The Four Horsemen are the bringers of the apocalypse. It was a warning to those who wanted to upset the balance," I said. Everyone knew that. I would've had to have lived under a rock not to.

"Not quite," Allistair said. A slow sensual smile lit his lips, making my cheeks heat. "We were never bringers of the apocalypse. We were the ones created to prevent it. Funny how history never seems to get that little detail right." He smirked at me, and I bit the inside of my cheek to stave off the lustful thoughts he was sending my way. The devil damned incubus knew exactly what he was doing.

"If you're not the bringers of the apocalypse, then who is?" I asked, trying to distract myself from the fuck me vibes he was sending.

"A few thousand years ago, there was a demon named Ragnarok who was gifted with premonitions. He saw the end of the world, as we knew it." He paused, letting a heavy silence fill in the gaps. "Humans have forgotten him, but remembered his vision. Ragnarok. The end of times.

"He said that one day the Horsemen would fail, and Lucifer would fall, and that when he did, the flames of Hell would go out. If the flames go out, then the gates of Hell open, leaving no barrier to stop all that lives in Hell from coming to earth," Julian said. "No barrier, that is, except Lucifer's child."

This is not the same version I was told as a child...

"Ragnarok prophesied that Lucifer would sire a daughter, and that she, and she alone, would be able to control the flames and stop the apocalypse, but it would be up to us to find her and bring her back." Julian took a deep breath. "Ragnarok's prophecy came true, Ruby. Lucifer died three days ago."

"*Died*? What do you mean he *died*?" I spluttered. "He's the fucking devil! The King of Hell. How the fuck does he just die?" Julian didn't bat an eyelash at my outburst. I don't think much phased him, but Rysten and Allistair shared a strained look. Laran's hands tightened, almost imperceptibly, were I not watching for it.

"To answer your question, love, he didn't. But that's a story for another time," Rysten interjected.

What the hell does that even mean?

I narrowed my eyes at him, not liking that answer, but knowing full well I had to accept it. Because what can you do? When the Four Horsemen are calling the shots, not a damn thing.

"The news of his death will trickle in over the coming weeks, and anarchy will ensue until the flames go out and Hell, for want of a better phrase, freezes over." Julian sensed my restlessness and stilled it. His eyes swirled with unnamable emotions and such a startling intensity that I almost didn't hear the second half of his statement. "We need you, Ruby. More than you know."

Whatever touching moment that might have been, stopped abruptly as I processed what was just said. They were deluded for thinking I was the devil's child, but they were abso-fucking-lutely insane if they thought I had the power to keep Hell in check. I could barely control my raccoon. The only gifts I'd expressed were that of a latent succubus, and I'd yet to transition. There was no way, not on this earth or in Hell, that I was destined to prevent an apocalypse.

"Look, I don't know whether you knew Lola or not, or what she may have said, but I have to be honest with you —I'm not the girl you're looking for," I said in a rush, setting my steaming cup of earl grey on the end table as I got to my feet. I crossed my living room and opened the front door. "I think it's best you leave."

Laran, the closest to me and the only one standing, narrowed his eyes. *War*. That's what the world called him. I could see it. He took a step closer, and I didn't move.

On the one hand, I didn't want to back down. That would make me look weak, and then they might not leave. On the other hand, he was now a lot closer than I wanted and I was well aware of the effect I had on men.

He leaned forward, so close that his breath caressed the sensitive part of my ear. I shivered as he whispered, "This isn't over, little succubus. We aren't going anywhere. Not without you. Don't even think about running. I like to chase."

His lips grazed the very corners of my ear and my breath hissed between my teeth. A zap of lightning went through me, making my blood sizzle. *What was that?*

"That's enough, Laran," Julian snapped. He pulled back a few inches, and I held my breath. His eyes had gone pitch black, blotting out any spec of color or trace of white. The air tasted thick with tension as he watched me for a heavy moment.

He's sizing me up. Full-blooded demons, and those who transition, have a harder time controlling our dark urges. I've been told the power can be maddening, and in some cases, consuming.

"War," Julian said sternly. This time someone physically grabbed him and pushed him towards the door. Laran growled under his breath and cast me one last heated look before leaving. I swallowed hard as Julian and Allistair followed. Rysten paused on his way out.

"I can't imagine this is easy to handle, love, but we will be here to help you through it," he said. I imagine most she-demons would fall all over themselves to hear those words from one of the Horsemen, but none of them were told they were supposed to take over the underworld.

"Please just go," I said. Rysten nodded in understanding and followed the others out into the night. I closed the door behind them and leaned against it. My legs gave out under me as I slid to the floor and Bandit came running out of my bedroom, his pink elephant in tow, stopping on my thighs to hold out his treasured toy.

"I don't think that's going to solve my problems this time, boy," I sighed. He kept pushing it towards me. I took the damn thing and held it while he climbed up my chest and wrapped his arms around my neck.

"Don't worry. I'm not leaving you. They can think I'm destined to be *Queen of the Underworld* all they want. It doesn't change anything." I don't know how much time passed until I dragged myself to bed, stripping off my blood-smudged clothes as I went.

LARAN

If Julian thought he could intimidate me into staying away from her, he was wrong. I'd waited just as long as the rest of them, and unlike Rysten, who went to her because Allistair called on him behind our backs, I stuck to the plan and didn't try to speak with her.

Until the plan changed.

I didn't mean to touch her.

I just couldn't think.

She was so close already, and she smelled *so good.* I've waited thousands of years to meet her, but the last twenty-three were the hardest.

The plan was to let Lola take her and not come back until it was time.

I waited. I paid my dues.

But she wanted nothing to do with us.

"Laran, you need to chill the fuck out, mate," Rysten snapped. I looked up at him and snarled, but the bastard didn't respond in kind. He rolled his eyes and continued sipping his wine, like he was classy or some shit. Fucking mommy drink is what that was.

Humans were making him soft.

"She wants nothing to do with us. How can you be sitting there like a fucking—"

"You think I haven't noticed? What did you expect, War? That we could come in here and usher her away? She doesn't know who you are. Who I am. She doesn't even know who *she is*. She only knows what earth has taught her."

I turned my back on him, towards the fire. Maybe I couldn't call the flames of Hell, but I could call on earth's fire and wreak havoc like the world has never known.

"Why does it feel like they took her from us?" I asked softly into the flames, but they held no answers for me this night.

"Because she created a life," Julian answered.

"This was what we wanted," Rysten continued.

"No," I said sharply. "This is what *you three* wanted. I wanted to keep her in Hell where—"

"Where she would have died with Lucifer," Julian interrupted.

I bit my tongue from the denial that threatened to come pouring out. He was right, but that didn't make this any easier.

"What are we supposed to do now?" I asked.

Silence spread between us, each lost to our own thoughts over the girl who was destined to be ours, but didn't know it.

Rysten was the first to speak. "We give her time and get to know her."

"I suggest we do this individually," Allistair proposed.

"So you can fuck her?" I asked. My words were harsh, but I meant it.

"I wasn't the one all over her tonight, War," he snapped back.

"You don't deny it."

"Enough," Julian declared. I turned away from the flames, toward my comrades. My brothers. We have stood together through everything. Fought and won for Hell itself. We have killed and laid destruction to so many in the name of the future. Of Ruby. Yet...this was different.

"Becoming her guards will be unlike any mission we have had before. It has already proven to have some challenges we hadn't predicted, and I think I can speak for all of us when I say we already feel a sense of entitlement to her," Julian said.

He wasn't wrong, and none of us corrected him.

"That being said, her well-being comes before anything we may want or feel. She's not comfortable with us yet, so we limit the time spent with her as a unit. At least until word from Hell reaches here. We can't postpone the inevitable. She must come with us, but we can give her time to adjust."

My gaze darted to Rysten. The fucker was practically smirking to himself at Julian's decree. He'd spent more time on earth than any of us over the last two decades, and while we all knew why, no one ever thought it might make a difference. We assumed she would want to come with us. That she would be happy to leave earth behind. We didn't take into account that she would grow up, have her own life, and become a woman in her own right, with sinful curves and a sultry mouth.

We didn't take *her* into account.

Just the idea of her.

All of us, but Rysten. The fucker was probably real happy right now, but he wasn't the only one with cards up his sleeve.

I am War, and no one plays better games than me.

CHAPTER 7

Groggy and exhausted, I woke to Moira screaming down the house. Not literally, but she may as well have been. I rolled over in bed and groaned. Bandit chittered about, jumping from his hammock hanging over my head and onto the floor. He paced wildly back and forth, scratching at the door.

"Ugh...why me?" I moaned, unwrapping myself from my sheets. I'd slept like the dead last night and woken up in a sheen of perspiration. I was going to need a shower before I went into the shop today.

Throwing open my bedroom door, I dragged my mostly naked ass into the living room. "What in the devil's name are you screaming about?" I asked, walking around the corner.

Rysten stood in the doorway with an extremely pissed off Moira. My best friend turned to respond, but lost the words once she saw me standing there in my underwear. I let out a frustrated growl and turned on my heel, ignoring the stark intensity that entered Rysten's expression. I wasn't a prude by any means, and took nudity in a pretty casual manner. Until you threw men into the mix. Bastards got a look of something they liked and never left me alone.

I dug through the never-folded pile of clean laundry sitting on the corner of my bed. At the very bottom was my black bathrobe. It was simple and cotton, definitely nothing sexy, and it would do the trick. I pulled on the robe and tied the sash at my waist as I walked back into the living room.

"Why is this asshole on our doorstep?" Moira demanded, like I was the one at fault.

"You think if I knew that I would've come around in my underwear?" I snapped back. She tilted her head to the side, narrowing her eyes as she considered that little detail for a moment before turning her anger back to him.

"What are you doing here, *boy*?" she asked him, not at all hiding her disdain at his presence. I nearly choked on the laugh that threatened to come out. Moira didn't know that Rysten was Pestilence. She didn't know he was a demon at all.

"I'm here to take Ruby to work," he said, not hiding his smirk.

"No, you're not," Moira answered for me.

"Hey," I protested. "I can answer for myself." Moira narrowed her eyes at me. *What's gotten into her lately?*

"Do you *want* him to take you to work?" she asked pointedly.

"Of course she does," Rysten responded before I could get a word in. I swung my glare in his direction. "Don't you, love?"

"No, I can't say that I do," I said hotly, stuffing my tongue in my cheek. I had mixed feelings where he and the others were concerned. It was my nature to want to play with fire, and four sexy and unbelievably powerful demons were just that. But. They also wanted to cart me off to Hell where I would probably die a terrible death once they realized they'd made a mistake.

"Now, love, I know this isn't easy on you, but—"

Rysten was still speaking when Moira slammed the door in his face.

"Why is he following you, Ruby?" she asked me, turning her back on the door. Rysten had gone quiet, but not for a second did I think he was actually gone. Not if they really believed what they told me, and given their behavior, I had no reason to think otherwise.

My eyes strayed to Moira and I gave her a noncommittal shrug. "You know how men are."

"I do," she said narrowing her eyes. "But he's not human, is he?"

Well, shit. Maybe she did know a thing or two.

"No," I said grimly. "He's not."

She nodded like that's what she expected. "Have you slept with him yet?"

"No. I haven't slept with any of them," I snapped, realizing a second too late that I just gave away more information than intended. *Shit.*

"Them?" she asked, raising an eyebrow. I rolled my eyes, letting out a sigh of exasperation. There was no way she was going to let it go now that I let that one slip. Great job, Ruby.

"You remember the guy who bailed me out of jail?"

She nodded slowly. "Well, he and Rysten work together with two other guys. The four of them came here for me because they have some crazy, delusional idea that I'm someone important. So, they think they need to protect me."

"Well, who do they think you are?" she asked, her voice filled with skepticism.

"Lucifer's daughter."

Silence ensued as we stared at each other until she burst out laughing. I waited for her to get her giggles out, and then she said, "That's a good one, but why are they really here?"

I stared blankly until her smile fell as the truth behind my words set in.

"They really believe you're the king's child?" she asked, like it only then occurred to her I might be telling the truth.

"It gets better," I said stiffly, and the whole story came pouring out of me. I collapsed on the sofa, all hope of making it into the shop early dissipated as I told her about the Horsemen and how they wanted to drag me back to Hell now that Lucifer died, all so I could somehow prevent the apocalypse from happening.

"Wow. I don't know what to say." Her voice was punctured by shock and disbelief.

"That makes two of us."

"What are you going to do?"

"I don't know, honestly. They wouldn't believe me when I told them they have the wrong person, but I have no intention of going to Hell just to prove them wrong." I picked at a piece of lint on my bath robe while Moira studied me.

"Are you sure..."

"Am I sure what?"

"Are you sure there's no way they may be right?"

I gaped at her, not even willing to entertain that thought. "Do you hear yourself right now? How is this even a question for you? You've known me most of your life. Have I ever come across as anything other than part-succubus?" My heart warbled in my chest while I spluttered the words.

"No," she exhaled. "But that doesn't mean you're not. There's always that chance your other half just hasn't manifested yet—"

"Do you really think that if Lucifer had a child, they wouldn't manifest before twenty-two?" I deadpanned.

Even she couldn't deny that. "Okay, so assuming you're not. What are you going to do about the Horsemen?" she asked as Bandit jumped onto the back of the couch and stuck his head through the blinds. Between the gap, I could see Rysten standing in the yard talking to someone on the phone.

"The way I see it, there isn't much I can do. They're going to follow me either way, and at least any other demons who think I'm Lucifer's daughter might leave me alone while they're around. I mean, they're bound to get the hint eventually, right?" I said throwing my arm over my face.

Moira shifted in her seat. "Hmm...possibly. They're demons, though, and when they take a liking to you..."

"That's an *if*, not a *when*," I pointed out, more for my

own peace of mind than anything. I was happy with my life here. I didn't want anything to change, but they made it clear they weren't leaving me alone, even if I wanted them to.

* * *

Bandit perched on my shoulder, munching on a carrot, as I walked out the front door. I'd been planning on leaving him at home today, but every time I reached for the doorknob, he tried to claw his way up my legs to come with me. Needy. I knew if I left him home, he'd tear everything to shreds just to get back at me. He was vindictive that way.

Rysten stood in my driveway, leaning against my car. His sand colored hair hung in his eyes and he had his arms crossed over his chest.

"I take it you four aren't leaving me alone anytime soon?" I asked as I approached the car. Rysten shook his head, the dark twinkle in his eye making my stomach do little summer saults.

"No can-do, love. You're stuck with us now that we've found you," he said, opening my driver's side door.

"You're not going to try to take my keys again, are you?" I asked warily.

He snorted. "I'm not Julian. Unlike Death, I realize that you're independent enough to chafe if we try to do everything for you," he said, a knowing twinkle in his eye. I swallowed hard and pretended not to notice the subtle brush of heat against my skin.

"Damn straight, I am." I stepped around him and

climbed in. The passenger side door opened, Rysten taking Bandit's seat. He growled under his breath at his usual space being occupied by this stranger, but he settled in the back of the car as I pulled out of the driveway.

"Your friend. She's not very fond of me, is she?" he asked. It was an abrupt change of subject. But given Moira's reaction to him on two occasions, I wasn't surprised he was curious.

"No. She's not very fond of most men who won't leave me alone," I said honestly.

"But I'm not a man," he pointed out.

"You're male and you've been stalking me. Close enough," I said with a roll of my eyes.

He chuckled under his breath, a dark and delicious sound. "It's good she's so protective of you," he said. "Even without being full-blooded succubus, I can feel the draw. A lesser demon would be hopeless to resist you." I swallowed hard, a question I shouldn't ask playing on the tip of my tongue. "You'll really be something when you come into your powers."

"*If* I come into my powers," I corrected. That earned another chuckle out of him.

"Oh, you will, love. Of that, I am certain." He sounded awfully confident for someone who was going to be hellaciously disappointed. I glanced sideways, but there wasn't a hint of the power or darkness I heard creeping into his voice. His glamor rippled when our eyes locked, and I quickly averted mine to the road.

"Why do you wear a glamor when the others don't?" I asked.

"Because the others are idiots in some regards," he said smugly.

"What do you mean?"

"What was your first thought when you met Allistair?" he asked. I thought of the brooding incubus. I'd known what he was from yards away, as much from the look in his eye to the way he moved. There was a raw power that radiated from him.

"He was"— I struggled to find a description that wasn't embarrassing, like sex-on-a-stick. That probably wouldn't earn me any points here—"intense."

Rysten nodded. "What about Julian?"

"Well, I shot him, so..."

"Exactly. And had you not met Laran when trying to get rid of your admirer"—his nose wrinkled in distaste–"you would have felt the same."

"That's one word for Josh."

"He's not worthy," Rysten said. Something about that response bothered me. It was almost territorial in a way, somehow implying *he* was worthy. I pulled into the parking lot behind the parlor and cut the engine.

Rysten brushed his thumb across his bottom lip, and I bit the inside of my cheek. While he was the most approachable of the Horsemen, he was still a demon, and a very powerful one at that.

"You still haven't answered my question," I said.

The corners of his lips turned up as he leaned forward. "Haven't I, love?"

My gaze went from his lips to his face, where his eyes gave away that very faint inkling of the darkness I sensed in him.

Realization dawned on me. "Because you think I'll let you get close to me just because you can make yourself seem more human."

His answering smile had me both pissed off and turned on. He leaned in, only inches from my face, and murmured, "That's what you're doing, isn't it?" His breath caressed my skin, drawing at the seductress within. I clamped down hard on my urges, fighting the lust unfolding inside me.

"No," I snapped, pulling back. "It's not."

I practically spun in my seat and wrenched the door open, jumping from the car to get as much space between us as possible. How could I have been stupid enough to ignore the obvious? I was more frustrated with myself than I was with him.

Bandit perched himself on the edge of the driver's seat and jumped towards me, wrapping his paws around neck. I put one arm underneath to support his weight and used the other to grip the car door.

Rysten tilted his head to the side as his glamor settled now that I wasn't so close. A boyish smile appeared on his lips as he said, "It's going to happen whether you like it or not, Ruby. You're ours to protect, and we take care of what's ours."

I slammed the car door and strode away from him as the reality of what it meant to have the Four Horsemen after me truly set in. This was going to be a long week. They would protect me from anything they saw as a threat because of who they thought I was.

But who would protect me from them?

CHAPTER 8

I WAS JUST CLOSING SHOP FOR THE WEEKEND WHEN the bell on the front door rang. I peeked my head around the corner and groaned when I saw who was standing there. It was none other than my lousy ex holding the sad makings of another apology in the form of a bouquet.

Why me?

"What are you doing here?" I asked. Bandit took one look at Josh and let out a growl. He held his head up higher at the sight of my raccoon. His posture couldn't have been straighter if someone shoved a pine tree up his ass.

"I came here to apologize for Sunday night." He motioned to the flowers in his hand. "I brought you daffodils. They're supposed to stand for forgiveness and new beginnings."

It took all my self-control not to gag. "I'm good. Thanks."

"Please, Ruby." *Devil save me, not the whining again.* I didn't have the patience for it today. I knew that it wasn't the loss of me that had him obsessing over our split. I knew it was the dormant succubus within. He had cheated on me claiming it was because I wouldn't sleep with him, but he also came groveling back every few days. It was exhausting. But sleeping with someone that didn't really give two shits about me, and had no choice, felt a little too much like rape. This is what I get for having *morals*.

"Please what?" I said, throwing my hands up in exasperation. "We broke up, Josh. I don't know what to say."

"That you'll forgive me and give me another chance—"

I held my hand up to stop him. "No. We are never, ever getting back together." I cringed as soon as the words were out, knowing I sounded like a bad Taylor Swift song.

"Is it because of those guys I saw with you? You have a"—he struggled with words for a moment, anger clouting his brain—"a *harem* now? Is that it?"

A harem? Now that's a thought. I was equally intrigued by the idea as I was pissed off by his attitude, given that he had absolutely zero reason to feel any sense of entitlement towards me. After all, his actions were what brought an abrupt end to our relationship, but with all the whining he was doing, I couldn't say I was sorry to see it end. At least I didn't have to feel bad about being bitchy this time.

"They have nothing to do with what happened between us, Josh. *You* are the one who cheated on *me*." I was beginning to sound like a broken record. This conversation was getting old, and fast.

"You wouldn't have sex with me! I waited months for you! Now you're sleeping with, what—three, four guys? But I'm willing to forgive you for your transgressions, if you can look past my small lapse in judgement."

Wow. I didn't even know how to respond. Unfortunately for him, he chose to be a total dick at the exact moment Laran was walking up. The door opened behind him, and he took one look over his shoulder and paled.

"I don't need your forgiveness because I don't want to be with you. Leave me alone," I said, hoping that Laran's presence would be enough to get him to go away.

Josh swallowed hard and uttered, "This isn't over. I will win you back." Delusional wasn't a strong enough word.

"Actually, you won't," Laran said darkly. "Stay away from Ruby, *boy*. My patience has an expiration, much like your life span." The menace in his voice wasn't soft or cunning. It was bold, and edged with a danger that just seemed to radiate from Laran. I'd only spoken with him briefly, less than the other three, and he scared the crap out of me. Josh would probably piss his pants if they kept this up.

"Are you threatening me?" Josh demanded. His face turned pink as he spluttered out his indignation.

"Yes." Laran stepped out of the way of the door, a not-so-subtle hint that it was time for him to leave.

Once again, Josh let out a string of curses, but did indeed storm off. The shop door slammed behind him, leaving me and Laran alone.

"Are all your exes this crazy?" he asked me. I guess at this point it was the closest we could get to small talk.

"Mostly," I responded. The ghost of a smirk crossed his lips, gone before I could tell if it was real.

"I guess that means I have my work cut out for me." He strode towards me like he owned the earth we walked on. Unapologetically and unequivocally male. My mouth dried as he neared me, but I didn't back away. The last thing I needed these demons thinking was that they could bulldoze me around.

"What are you doing here?" I asked, fidgeting with the corner of my sleeve. Strangely enough, Bandit stayed quiet as he approached me. Unlike Josh, whom he had always disliked, he didn't seem to care one way or the other if Laran was near me. I wasn't sure if I should find that comforting, or worrisome.

"It's my turn," he said proudly.

"Your turn?"

"To spend time with you," he clarified. I frowned. *They were taking turns on who—*

"Who says I want to spend time with you?" I didn't particularly care for being told what to do or who I would spend time with.

"Would you rather Allistair or Julian?"

"Um..." My non-answer must have been answer enough.

He smirked and held out his hand. "Come. I promise not to bite. *This time.*"

This time? I licked my bottom lip at the promise in those words. I wasn't supposed to be attracted to them, or at the very least, not playing out my fantasies, but I couldn't help but wonder what Laran might taste like.

Just a bite. He was a full-grown male demon, well into his prime, and the things he could teach me...

My wishful thinking stopped as memories knocked me back to reality. It'd been a long, long while since I got laid, thanks to what happened last time. Seeing as I had no immediate plans to fix that, I just accepted that I was damned if I did, and damned if I didn't.

Taking a deep breath, I said, "Fine, but I need to drop Bandit off at home first. He doesn't like people, and humans are prejudice dicks."

Laran gave me a savage grin. "Who said anything about humans?"

I wasn't sure if I should be excited or concerned at the prospect of whatever the Horseman of War had planned. The demonic glint in his eye should have been all the warning I needed.

Half an hour after dropping Bandit at home, we pulled of the highway. A 'Keep Out' sign sat just before the bend in the road that turned and revealed this run-down lot in the middle of nowhere. The bits and pieces of trash scattered about would have made it look like any other abandoned lot you find, had conifers not towered over the make-shift building, keeping it hidden from unwanted eyes. It looked like a great location for a horror movie. In front of a rickety shed made of plywood was a moderate plot of compacted dirt, currently being used as a parking lot for the few cars parked outside. Spray-painted lines marked the spots where cars were supposed to park, not that it seemed the drivers paid that any mind. The slightly bent brambles and flattened grass were the only indication that an unmarked road existed just off the highway that led here. There was just something too convenient about that, and it didn't sit right with me.

I suddenly felt like we were about to walk into the middle of some shady shit.

"Where are we?" I asked as we got out of the car. An upside-down pentagram hung from the top of the lopsided door, the only indication about what might await me inside.

"I thought I'd take you on a little field trip. Get you away from all the heaviness of this past week," he replied without hesitation. I faltered mid-step, tripping over a rock because I was too busy looking at him. My arms flailed as I started to fall towards the ground, but Laran caught me by the elbow. Swift. Firm. He pulled me back so I didn't fall flat on my face, or through the uneven door.

"That's oddly considerate for a demon. The Horseman of War, no less," I murmured. Laran stepped closer and bent down, his lips grazing my jaw.

"Haven't you heard the saying, *all is fair in lust and war*?" he whispered. I shivered at the brush of his lips against that sensitive place just beneath my ear.

"I'm pretty sure the saying is *love and war*," I responded dryly. His lips curved up against my skin, leaving a trail of heat in their path.

"I like my version better," he rumbled. His very demeanor called to me, dark and seductive. Like a moth to a flame. But a moth didn't realize it was going to get burned. I was smart enough to know, and part of me wanted it. A small sadistic side of me was drawn to these men—to all men—and it had nothing to do with love, or war.

I swallowed hard, shoving my inner she-demon back. She was going to get me into trouble if she had her way.

Laran chuckled as I stepped away from him, but didn't release his hold on my elbow. His fingers were distracting, but I didn't complain as he pushed open the lopsided door and escorted me into what was, for all intents and purposes, a dive-bar. For demons.

All eyes turned on us and I froze.

Why the fuck would he take me to a bar for demons in the middle of nowhere? He may as well have offered me up to them on a silver platter and said bon appétit.

"What are we doing here, Laran?" I hissed through gritted teeth. I moved to shrug off his grip, but he held me tighter.

"Relax, Ruby. They don't know who I am. Anyone who looks at me will just see a glamor of a male demon they won't want to fuck with, and by extension, you." I stared up at him, my gaze slowly falling to the hand possessively wrapped around my arm. He was...laying a claim on me. A warning to anyone thinking they might want a new plaything. He was letting them know I am not on the market.

I let loose a shaky breath as he moved us further into the bar. The scent of smoke and citrus drifted over me and my muscles relaxed instantly. I inhaled deeply, the softest of sighs escaping my lips as the tension left me altogether.

"Feeling better?" Laran asked. His lips twitched in an amused smirk.

"Much," I answered through the haze that was beginning to cloud over. The corners of my vison softened, but the world never seemed so bright. So...tempting. My inner seductress smiled at the crowded bar as I walked away from Laran and squeezed my way in between two mischievous looking males.

"I'll have a Black Russian on the rocks. Make it a double." My voice came out sultry. The succubus was out to play.

LARAN

She disappeared.

One minute she was standing next to me, sexy little smile lighting up her face, and the next minute she was gone. Someone was going to fucking pay for this, and it wouldn't be pretty.

A barely-tempered fury pounded in my chest as I scanned the gambling tables. Imps of every shape and size, banshees of all colors, a Chupacabra here and there, even a few shades littered the crowd, but no Ruby. Her amaryllis and lavender scent filled the air, mixing with the pungent smoke of burning white lotus. White lotus: the drug of choice for most demons, and a far kinder version of the black lotus that was known for its...undesirable effects.

I left the gambling tables and searched the bar where I picked up the briefest hint of her. She was close, and yet, as I searched the entirety of the bar, I couldn't find her anywhere. *How the fuck did I lose her? The only person in the world I was created to protect?*

This shit was unbelievable.

The itching inside me that something had gone terribly wrong sped up as I barreled toward the stairs. If I found her in one of these back rooms tied up like—I couldn't even finish that thought. If she was up here, someone was going to die. I squared my jaw and kicked open the first door I saw.

A sallow-cheeked she-demon looked up at me and let out a purr while the male behind her continued pounding into her flesh. She was bent over a desk that had seen better days. Her feral grin and crooked finger she used to try to beckon me forward was not appetizing in the slightest. There was only one person I felt like slamming my cock into and it wasn't the drugged-out whore before me. I didn't bother with closing the door as I moved on to the following rooms. They were all much the same: she-demons with one or two males, and no Ruby.

I ran a hand through my hair as I paced the balcony overlooking the bar.

Where the fuck was she?

Nearly half an hour had passed since we walked into The Black Brothers and there was still no sign of her. Much longer and I was going to need to scour the grounds to see if someone snuck her out. I would have thought she would put up enough of a fight, but I didn't get the vibe she was used to smoking white lotus, and the room itself was a hefty dose that left even the stronger demons slightly delirious.

She's young. She hasn't transitioned. What the fuck was I thinking bringing her here?

I took one last round of the bar before my patience ran out. She was here somewhere. I could smell it, but someone was glamoring her.

"Allistair, I need you to get your ass down to Black Brother's. Ruby's missing."

Under any other circumstances, I would chew my own arm off before I called on one of the other Horsemen. Glamors weren't my specialty, though, and there was no way I was calling on Julian for this. People always thought I was the biggest, baddest fucker around, but that's only because they'd never seen Death in action. Truth be told, you were already a goner if you saw him lift a finger in a fight. His particular brand of subtly was not needed for this, and Rysten had already pissed me off too much this week. I didn't know what state Ruby would be in when we found her, but I would rather place my pride on Allistair's help than the doom-and-gloom twins.

"How the fuck did you lose her?" His response took longer than I'd hoped, given who we were talking about.

"Someone fucking glamored her and is hiding her underneath my nose. I need you to sniff the fucker out," I snapped back.

"I'm on my way." Thank the fucking devil for that. I needed him here yesterday.

I didn't want to check the clock, but I knew the time was racking up. I gripped the railing, not noticing that I'd burned most of it away before I began to stumble over the edge. I pushed a gail of wind up from the floor below, and it hoisted me back onto the upper platform as parts of the broken railing fell on the poker table below. So much for keeping my cool.

I could burn the building down. Tear through it with a twister unlike any other. Flood it with rain that would drown half of the demons in this room. Even decimate it with an earthquake that would level all of Portland.

But Ruby was in here somewhere, and I needed to get my shit together until I found her.

Allistair came striding through the door in record time. Famine must have been staring at himself in the mirror when I reached out, given how quickly he got here. I was halfway down the stairs when his eyes locked on something. I hoped to Satan it was Ruby, because if it wasn't, I would level the Black Brothers to the fucking ground.

"Laran," Allistair said. The surrounding demons gave a wide berth when they realized who my friend was. I dropped my own glamor and the bar went silent. All except for one.

Allistair snapped his fingers, and disintegrated her glamor. Across the bar at the very first table I checked, was Ruby.

She was sitting on an imp's lap, letting out breathy little gasps.

Air tunneled through the bar at my beck and call, winking out the fire that burned the lotus leaves. The imp's hands crept tighter around her, pulling her supple skin closer to his body. The look on her face was dazed and confused.

He *dared* to conceal a claimed she-demon?

I saw red, and it was war.

CHAPTER 9

THE MALE ON MY LEFT TURNED TO ME AND SAID, "Strong drink. What's your name, dollface?"

I gave him an appraising look. Neatly kept dark hair framed a handsome face. His eyes were wicked red and his teeth unnaturally white. He had a mischievous look about him, and I instantly put together that he was an imp. One of the most common demons in these parts, but also the ones a succubus would least want to tango with, if she were thinking clearly. I most certainly, was not.

A full-blooded imp has some impressive powers to any lesser demon, but lesser I was not. Even a half-breed like me would be a prize in a place like this. Our skin was the most potent aphrodisiac on the planet, ten times more so to other demons.

It was why I'd always stayed away. For fear of what someone skilled in persuasion, or Hell forbid, blood magic, could do.

But for the first time in my existence, I did not feel afraid. On the contrary, his enigmatic persona was drawing me in, and he hadn't said more than six words. Either he was more skilled with persuasion than even I could have guessed, in which case I was already fucked, or I was a glutton for punishment. Given how he exuded confidence like some men wore their desperation, I was inclined to believe it was a bit of both.

How lucky for me.

I eyed the black edges of a brand that were simultaneously peeking out of his collar and the cuff on his wrist. The ink was white, not the traditional black. Somewhere in the back of my mind, that meant something. So did the edges of what appeared to be flowers petals, but for the life of me, I couldn't seem to hold onto that thought, that concern, for more than a moment before I relaxed back into a state of forgetfulness. My heart rate slowed to a steady thump, falling in line with the rhythmic beat of a song only I could hear. I smiled coyly to the imp as the bartender slid my drink to me and said, "It's on the house."

I turned my pretty little smile on the bartender and he gave me a wink as I accepted the Black Russian and walked away from the bar. The imp would follow. I was sure of it. For a brief moment, I wondered where Laran went, but as I approached the table where the smoke was coming from, I seemed to no longer care.

All thoughts of Laran, the Horsemen, and even thoughts of myself vanished as I stood over the crowded gambling table. Dice and cards were flying everywhere, but the slow burning pot in the center made it hard to tear my gaze away.

"You want dealt in, poppet?" someone called out from the other side of the table. I shook my head.

"Can I watch?" I heard the soft, velvety purr in my voice. The males at the table looked up at me, and the scraping of a chair made me turn. The imp from the bar had pulled up a seat, and the others moved to make room for him. He lithely sat down in the chair, his knees parted as he leaned back and beckoned me.

"If you're sitting on my lap, you can," he growled. My stomach tightened at the challenge in his voice. I strode up to him and threw my head back, finishing my Black Russian in one swallow. I slammed the cup on the table and turned my body around to perch on his knees. The imp took my invitation for what it was and placed a hand on my waist. Something like obsession took me as I focused on the funny looking leaves in the pot. The edges curled slowly, burning bright. I watched them, in a state of suspended euphoria that didn't seem to have a beginning or end. It just was, and I existed within it.

The imp flexed his fingers, the claw tips biting into my skin just beneath the sweater. I let out a sigh and shifted back. Closer to the demon. To heat. His arm wound around my waist, and I parted my legs so he could pull me back. Flush against him, I could hardly contain the moan building in my throat. Devil have me, I wanted him. I wanted all of them. I wanted to feel something heavy and hard between my legs, placating the need that drove me.

The imp's other hand clamped down on my knee that was pinned between his legs. Hot and heavy, his breath made my flesh break out in goosebumps as he whispered, "What do you want, dollface?"

I squirmed restlessly on his lap as his hand unsheathed its claws and slowly started the ascent up my leg, dipping into the jagged rips in my dark jeans. A sigh escaped my lips as the hand around my waist tightened, and his fingers slipped under my shirt. The brush of his claws made me ache and my back arched—

"Get your fucking hands off of her."

The hands on my body froze and I let out a hiss. That was not part of the deal. I turned my hooded eyes up to the demon that dared interrupt us, but was not prepared to see Laran and Allistair standing there.

Laran's face was a mask of frozen fury. I shivered leaning back into the demon whose lap I was currently sitting on. He didn't feel so hot anymore, and the ache I was feeling was on the cusp of pleasure and pain.

"Famine. War, I'm sorry. I didn't realize who you—"

"Ruby. Come," Allistair commanded. My eyes swiveled from the glowering demon threatening to explode, to the demon striding towards me with a voice that my made my stomach jerk. He reached out with both hands and plucked me from the imp's lap, locking one arm under my knees and supporting my back with the other. I squirmed in his grip, but Allistair held tight.

"Save your words, imp. You glamored her and tried to separate us after I placed my claim." Laran's voice boomed, shaking the tables enough that glass rattled against the countertops of the bar and shattered as it fell to the earth. In my delirious state, I couldn't process what was happening, or why. I just felt the need that drove me.

I leaned into Allistair and inhaled deeply. Smoke filled my lungs, making me burn at my very core; a raging inferno that would not be denied.

"I'm taking her home, Laran. Make sure you clean up your mess."

Laran grunted in response and Allistair began moving. We crossed through the bar, moving faster and farther from the smoke with every second. I watched over Allistair's shoulder as we crossed the threshold, the embers on the smoking leaves expiring, and then we were gone.

One moment we were outside the bar, standing in the parking lot, and the next we were in an oddly familiar bathroom. Home, I recognized, as he opened the bathroom door connected to my bedroom. My queen-sized bed loomed in front of us and all I could hear, all I could feel, was the heat radiating through him. I turned my face towards his, biting my lip when I saw the fevered intensity. His eyes were not just amber. They were molten gold. He was angry, but I couldn't register why.

Only that I knew I wanted to take it away.

As my back hit the bed, and Allistair started to pull away, I fisted his shirt in my hand, holding him there.

"Stay." It was a single word: a command, a request, a plea, but it reverberated across the room and over his skin. I bit my lip again as his eyes dilated and darkened. He leaned forward, drawn in by the effect I had on him as I pushed my need through the air, through his clothes, over his skin, and into him.

"Ruby," he growled. The pain in his voice echoed the burning between my legs. I tugged him closer, grabbing his shirt with both fists and pulling. The buttons popped and ripped open when he stopped only inches away. I let out a growl and reached again, tearing through the undershirt. The moment our skin came into contact, an intense current of electricity shocked me, only it didn't hurt. But the burning beneath my skin didn't subside. A lust like I'd never known owned me.

"I need you," I whispered. The craving shook my body so hard, I was trembling. Allistair hovered over me, looking me up and down as I cocked my head, the succubus inside of me knowing just how to play the man before me.

"It's the drugs," he growled, the muscles in his arms flexing as he held himself inches away from me.

"I don't care. It hurts," I mewled. Allistair's eyes flashed and he took a tight breath before a resolution seemed to settle over him. He moved back to step away as I quickly sat forward to stop him. He wrapped his hands around my wrists, holding me at arm's length, but making no move to let me go. Gently, he pushed me until my back touched the bed and released my arms with a strained kind of control.

"I'm going to make it go away, Ruby, but you have to do what I tell you," he murmured. I nodded as he removed his suit jacket and ripped shirts. I gripped the sheets as I drank in his very scent, waiting for him. Admiring the shape of him, the ripples of his muscle, the contours of his abdomen traveling below the line of his belt...he settled on his knees in front of me and motioned for me to sit up again. I hated being told what to do, but the throbbing ache between my legs was not going anywhere.

Slowly, he hooked his fingers under the corners of my sweater and pulled it off. The crisp air hit my flesh and I let out a gasp. He placed a single finger against my lips, instructing me to keep quiet. Knowing it was rebellious, I opened my mouth and bit his finger as he let out a sharp hiss. Without warning, I was on my back, legs dangling over the edge of the bed, my jeans ripped off. I tried to sit up, but he forced me to my side, pinning both arms above my head as he lay next to me.

"Let me—"

"Shhh..." he whispered in the hollow of my ear. His other hand gripped my hip and began caressing my skin, teasing me as he moved his hand up my body.

"I'm not going to have sex with you, Ruby. Not tonight. You will barely remember, and I want you to remember the first time I make you scream." He squeezed my hardened nipples through the soft cotton of my bra. Pulling down the cup, he freed my breast to the chilled air and locked his deft fingers around my taut peak, rolling his thumb to send a sharp pleasure shooting through me. I let out a low moan as his lips brushed over my neck, and a throaty growl escaped as he bit me hard, sending shocks through my body.

"I'm not even going to kiss you," he continued. He moved his hand from my breast and trailed it down, grazing lightly over my ribs and settling on the apex of my thighs, cupping me over my cotton underwear.

"But I will take care you. I'm going to take the hurt away, Ruby, but no more," he whispered against my bare shoulder as his fingers rubbed over my sex. My head lolled as I arched into him.

"Please," I moaned. Allistair bit into me harder, and I let out a sharp yelp. It broke the skin, but it felt so good. I pushed against his hands, but he wasn't having it.

"I am going to let you go. And you will do as I say if you want your release. Is that understood?"

I whined in answer.

"Promise me, Ruby. Say you'll be good and you'll do as you are told."

Every part of me aching for his touch, I nodded and breathed out, "I promise. Just...please."

Allistair pulled away from me, his commanding presence dictating my every move so that I could have the one thing I wanted. He told me to sit up. I sat. He told me to move to the center of the bed. I moved. He told me to lay down on my side. I did as I was told. Allistair climbed in beside me and pressed my back to his front, positioning his arm underneath the curve in my side to wind it around my waist and shackle both my arms simultaneously. I writhed in the constriction.

"Shhh...you promised you would be good." He slipped his free hand down my hip and into my panties. I opened my legs as far as being spooned against him would allow me, and he took the invitation. He parted my folds with his fingers, grazing my clit just enough to make me buck. Impatient, I ground back into his hips, driven by the feel of his cock against my backside. He was impossibly hard, and yet, he wouldn't have me. I grit my teeth as I rubbed against him.

He hissed, and his fingers stopped.

Something dark and ugly unfurled in my chest, but I kept it in and stopped all movement. His fingers continued. I tried to keep my moans from escaping as he slipped a single finger inside of me, the slickness of my desires coating him. My body was begging for more, but he was drawing this out.

I shifted again, grinding against him. Again, he stopped.

"I'm not going to fuck you, Ruby. You take what I give, or you get nothing at all," he growled. Power lashed out from him, for just a moment, but it forced me to be still. The moment I stopped, he slipped two fingers inside of me, gliding them back and forth, pressing his palm into the swollen, sensitive nub. I arched my hips, trying to move against his fingers. Feel them deeper. Faster. Allistair's grip didn't give my body a single inch of room to chase my own pleasure the way I wanted. He kept at a slow torturous assault, letting an intense ache build inside of me that only he could relieve.

"More," I whispered, but I didn't dare rock back into him. Not when I was so close. I was so fucking close. He would reward me...

The force of his palm against my clit, rubbing it in rhythmic circles, faster... his fingers sweeping, plunging deep inside me...the pressure building, twitching, and burning as his speed increased...

"Come for me, Ruby," Allistair commanded. He left a trail of suckling kisses down my neck as I found my release. Stars exploded behind my eyes, so violent and so sudden that I couldn't scream. Waves of pleasure crashed through my body as I poured. I couldn't do anything but ride it out as I shuddered, his fingers never ceasing, working me all the way.

The moment my orgasm stopped, he pulled his hand away and clarity started to fill my mind. I twisted, trying to turn towards him, but his hard, unyielding body kept me trapped how he wanted me.

"Sleep," he whispered. The sound of his heart beating was the last thing I heard before the world faded black and sleep overcame.

ALLISTAIR

I didn't know if I was a Devil damned saint, or the worst fucking piece of shit in her life right now. No, I couldn't be the worst. Laran now held that title, thanks to his little excursion tonight. A low growl slipped from my throat before I could cut it off. Even in her sleep, she arched into me. Wanting something I very much planned to give her.

Soon. Just not tonight.

She wouldn't remember everything the white lotus brought on, but she would remember enough. I was not taking advantage of her when she was high. That would be fucking despicable, even for me.

My cock twitched as she moved closer, completely unaware of the effect she had on me. Well, not completely. She thought she was keeping her distance this past week. Ignoring me as best she could. What she didn't realize was that I could see that glint of need in her eyes every time she looked at me. I could feel it, as sharp and painful as I felt my own.

The only difference was that I wouldn't make her

suffer because of Laran's fuck up. Even if it made it harder for me to stay away and keep my hands off of her. Julian's rules could go fuck themselves.

He could spout honor and duty as much as he wanted, but I knew the truth.

He wanted her just as bad as the rest of us. He just wouldn't give in.

I wasn't nearly as selfless, or stupid. It's what kept me here, in her bed. When I knew I should have left. She was a temptation; not quite forbidden, but entirely unexpected. When Lucifer brought us forth from the flames and gave us our purpose, I never imagined that I would want to fuck her like I do now.

I was supposed to protect her from men like me. Like Laran. Like Rysten. Especially Julian.

She wasn't a child though, and I never knew the child she was. The babe I saw all those years ago was gone. A week ago, I thought I hated myself for it because I missed out on knowing her. What I really hated was that I wanted her. If I'd been here when she was a child, that would have never come to pass. I wouldn't be in her bed right now, contemplating all the ways I was going to fuck her.

There was no going back now, not when her lips had my mind painting pictures of her on her knees. Putting her smart mouth to much better use.

Her dark blue hair slid across my chest as she twisted around in her sleep. So beautiful. So unique. She thought that we had the wrong girl, but never before have I met someone with hair the color of the flames. Not even Lucifer. I slid my hand through the slippery strands, mesmerized by the color change. The blue was dark enough to pass for black, until the light reflected the most stunning of azures.

"Where is she?" Laran's presence brushed against my mind, uninvited.

"She's at home. What do you want?" I replied tersely, brushing my fingers across the curve of her neck. The skin was so soft. Supple. A breathy little moan escaped her lips.

"I'm going to stop by and check on her. Can you tell Jul—"

"There's no need. I'm here with her." I sent back, focusing on the girl before me. They would call me away soon, but I didn't want to move. Not yet. Not when tomorrow was already coming.

"Why are you still with her?" There was a challenge in his tone. I frowned in annoyance, running my hand over the curve of her hip.

"Because she was so fucking high on white lotus, she may have hunted down the first man on the street to sate her if I hadn't made her go to sleep," I snapped back. There was no need to mention what happened before she went to sleep. Not even I would have been strong enough to calm her had I not given her what she needed first. She was the strongest succubus I had encountered pre-transition. The oldest, too. She was using powers she shouldn't have before the change, and starving herself while she did it, no less. I don't know what went down in her past, but something happened that made her hesitant with men. Male demons even more so. Her body was begging to be touched and fulfilled, but her mind wanted no part of it.

Not consciously anyway.

"Meet me back home. Rysten is on his way to watch her." A sudden flash of anger boiled within me at his blatant attempt to get me away from her. He even went so far as to call in Rysten, who he hadn't bothered with at the bar. The fucker needed to remember it was his carelessness that caused this, and I had just as much right to her as he did.

"Feeling a bit heavy-handed, War?" I mentally growled back, sending my displeasure along with it. Ruby winced against me, pushing back. Her mind lashed out with power like an iron lifted right out of flame. It speared through my shields without effort, and took a sharp stab at the innermost part of myself. Attacking, where no demon had ever held the power to before. I recoiled from her, catching myself as I toppled out of her bed.

Had she felt my displeasure? Had that made her lash out? Or was it something more?

Even more curious, was where that power came from when she'd never given a hint of it before. I knew that something lurked inside her, as it had her father. I was almost certain that was not it, but something else entirely.

I watched her for a moment longer, the blood in my veins calling me back to her bed. As much as I didn't want to, I needed to get back and report what just happened.

It appeared our girl had more to her than meets the eye.

CHAPTER 10

The birds were chirping. The bees were buzzing. It was Saturday morning, and I didn't have work. The pounding in my head served as a reminder for the bad choices I made the night before. Like letting Laran take me to a demon bar, and getting felt up on some creepy imp's lap. Oh, and let's not forget how I finished the night off by throwing myself at Allistair.

Yeah. Last night was a shit show by anyone's standards.

I wanted to yell at Laran and blame him for putting me in the situation to begin with, but he didn't really make me go. He didn't make me high. I'm also equally sure he didn't make me seduce Allistair. All of which meant that as much as I wanted someone to blame, this was all on me, and it fucking sucked.

Being a demon and having lowered inhibitions wasn't always fun, compared to what people might think. At the end of the day, or really, the next morning, we still had to wake up and deal with the consequences.

"I'll have four orders of bacon and a cup of coffee. Thanks, Martha."

Yep. My consequences were me hiding in Martha's Diner and treating myself to bacon while I sat at my usual booth and stewed about the bad life choices I'd made. I liked to pretend it was a pre-reward for when I chose to do the right thing next time, but honestly, it was just another Saturday morning, and that meant this booth was the only place my ass would be.

The jingle of the bell on the front door pulled me from my inner rambling. *Please don't be Kendall.* I was not in the mood to deal with her shit today. By the time my head swiveled around to check the door, the shift in power that was seeping through the room left little guesswork about who it was.

Golden eyes bore into mine and the sinking feeling in my stomach became an anchor tugging me to the linoleum floor. I wanted to evaporate on the spot, but not even disappearing would save me from the embarrassment of last night. I straightened my spine and kept my head high.

"I went by your shop, but you're closed on Saturdays," he stated. He wasn't loud, but he projected enough that I heard him from across the diner. Devil damn him. Between Allistair and Kendall, the Saturday crowd would not be happy with me. I chose to ignore him, but I knew he wouldn't go away. "What kind of tattoo artist are you? That doesn't make a lot sense."

"It's the one day I have off, and it has been that way since I started taking care of myself. Now, if you'll excuse me..." I let me voice trail off, making it abundantly clear that I wanted him to leave. Silly me, thinking one of the Horsemen knew how to take a hint.

"Rather limiting, don't you think?" he continued, crossing the diner in smooth, measured steps. I growled under my breath, but shoved down the urge to throw a salt shaker at his head.

"If someone wants a tattoo, they can come in the other six days of the week. I'm not staying open until two in the fucking morning on a Saturday for drunk rejects to stumble in and get something they'll regret in the morning. That's not how I run my business, and it's a great way to tarnish your name." I leaned back in the booth and crossed my arms over my chest.

"If you say so," he said when he reached the table. He placed a hand on my shoulder and I slapped it away instantly, like he was an annoying fly and not someone whose every movement I was keenly aware of.

"What do you want?" I snapped at him. Allistair grinned at me, like he knew *exactly* where my thoughts had been going.

"You," he said bluntly without having the decency to keep his voice down. The fucking audacity. I swallowed hard, pleased that the vixen inside me was stomped on by a sizzling anger racing through me. I opened my mouth to tell him off, but he put a finger to my lips in the most publicly sexual way possible. "Now, now, Ruby. No need to make a scene. It is my turn after all."

I considered biting him just to prove a point, but the coughing behind him and the smell of bacon brought me to a halt. Allistair stepped aside and took the seat across from me as Martha sat down my pile of bacon and a cup of steaming black coffee.

"There a problem here, Ruby?" Martha asked. Her sharp brown eyes cut towards Allistair. It wouldn't have been the first time some jackass wouldn't leave me alone. If only Allistair was a stalker. He wasn't though, and even if Martha threw him out, I know he would just find me later. Better now in a public setting where he couldn't try any funny business.

"I'm good, Martha. Thanks," I said. She watched him for a moment longer before turning to me.

"If you need anything, just holler. Ol' Ben keeps a baseball bat in the back just for the persistent ones." I choked on my sip of coffee, silently waving her off. She threw Allistair one last look of disdain before leaving us.

"The old woman thinks you need protection from me," Allistair noted as I took a swig of my coffee.

"Do I?"

Allistair's eyes flickered with something akin to amusement, but that wasn't all that was lurking there. The onyx flecks swirled around the iris; mesmerizing, but deadly. Allistair was the Horsemen of Famine, and as far as I could tell, the strongest incubus I'd ever come across. He said he was here to protect me, but my hazy memories from the night before didn't lend to that. There was a darkness in his eyes, something so sharp and painful, but in the most pleasurable of ways. A predator. I had no desire to be his prey.

"You have nothing to fear from me. I make no guarantees for the rest of this world, but I would never harm you," Allistair said.

"Because you think I'm Lucifer's daughter?"

Allistair narrowed his eyes and replied, "You are his daughter. I have no doubt about that." His smug voice and cold arrogance was off-putting. I pursed my lips, taking another sip of coffee.

"My birth certificate is hardly proof," I scoffed. I'd always hated having the last name Morningstar, but in a world full of humans, most people didn't know how odd it was to be a demon named after the king himself. Not once in my almost twenty-three years have I ever questioned there being more to it, and given my lackluster abilities, I wasn't about to start.

"Your birth certificate is just what we used to track you. We didn't need it to prove who you were. We know who you are. We've always known. We were there the day you were born. We were there when Lola smuggled you out of Hell. Rysten's the one that made your birth certificate while Lucifer placed his mark on you. You grew up invisible because we needed you to." The controlled passion that lay beneath that smooth, honey-like voice silenced me. I didn't know how to reply, because I didn't know if he was telling the truth. He sounded like he was sincere, but I wasn't dumb enough to trust my instincts. Demons lie. They cheat. His abilities alone could probably make me believe the sky was yellow if I gave him the chance. There was also a hole in his story...

"I don't have a mark."

Allistair's eyes dropped to my chest and back up. If I didn't know any better, I'd say he was checking me out. I opened my mouth to tell him where his eyes belong—

"Ruby!"

Fuck me. I knew that voice. It belonged to the only person in Portland that could make me cringe out of both pity and annoyance.

"Kendall," I muttered under my breath, rolling my eyes. I took a long drink of my coffee, hoping she would see I was with someone and leave. Unfortunately, that was not the case.

"What are you doin' here? You should be banned from comin' here after what you did to my car," she sneered as she stomped toward our table.

"I don't know what you're talking about," I feigned innocently as I schooled my face into a bored expression. Her brown eyes sparkled with hatred until they turned to the person sitting across from me. I didn't know if it was because Allistair exuded sex appeal, or if she really couldn't stand to see any man near me, but her eyes roamed over his designer suit and dark hair, turning more lustful and jealous by the second. *Oh, boy. Here we go.*

"Who might you be?" she inquired, waiting for his name. There was a subtle coax to her voice that I think was meant to be alluring, but instead made her sound desperate. Allistair tore his eyes from my face to give her a dismissive glance.

"I'm a friend of Ruby's," he said coldly. I wasn't sure whether I was supposed to do a little clapping dance in my head, or be concerned by the venomous glare she turned back to me.

"I'd be careful keepin' company with a girl that has her *record*. She's goin' to find herself in such trouble one day that even the Lord can't save her from it," Kendall said. Her words were meant to be chilling, but her implied threat didn't worry me.

"You can't save someone that's already damned," I muttered under my breath.

"Are you admittin' your indiscretions?" Kendall said tersely.

"Only if you admit yours." She blanched on the spot and I cocked an eyebrow.

"I don't know what you're talkin' about," she said stiffly. I munched obnoxiously on a piece of bacon because I knew it annoyed her.

"Isn't that my line?" I shot back, hiding my grin behind the lip of my coffee cup. She narrowed her eyes, smoothing over her yellow dress. Always so prim and proper in front of people.

"I have no idea what Josh ever saw in you," she said snidely.

"Self-respect and pure fucking awesomeness," I deadpanned. Kendall's mouth set in a firm line, and while it was mildly amusing to push her buttons, I wanted her to leave.

"My lawyer will be in touch," she said grimly. She started to turn away when Allistair thrust out his hand. She froze mid-turn and glanced back.

"Be sure to give him my card. I'll be representing her from now on," Allistair said in a voice devoid of any warmth. I was a bit shell-shocked myself, given that I didn't think he was a real lawyer, or would be suitable representing me for a damn parking ticket, much less arson. I wasn't going to say that in front of her, though.

Her perfectly manicured nails, extending like claws as she took the card and turned those hateful eyes on me.

"I'd be careful who you sleep aroun' with for favors, Ruby. By the looks of him, I think you've bitten off more than you can chew," she said with a cunning smile.

"Thanks for the concern, but I think I'll be just fine. A little whipping never hurt anybody," I snapped. The words were out of my mouth before I could think about it.

Kendall's face flamed red as she turned and marched out of the diner muttering "*Satanists*" under her breath. The diner went oddly quiet as the other customers pretended to be absorbed by the daily news or a speck of lint on their shirts. Even up at the counter, Martha was taking her time ringing up orders, albeit with a grin on her face. I drained the rest of my coffee as Allistair let out a chuckle under his breath.

"You know, I'm not one for whipping, but I'm sure Julian would be happy to oblige if you—"

"Stop talking."

"Is there something else you would rather do?" he asked, the wicked glint in his eyes making my stomach clench.

"Not with you."

"That's not what you were saying last night," he mused. I pinned him with a hard glare even though I felt dirty inside. Dirty because I liked what I remembered. I liked it a lot, but neither of us were in our right minds when we did it.

"That won't happen again. You can thank Laran and the Black Brothers for that one," I muttered.

Allistair watched me for another moment. "Perhaps. But we have an eternity together, and I look forward to every minute of it once you realize that." His words sent shivers down my spine, both good and bad.

I should have heeded my own warning about playing with fire.

CHAPTER 11

The sharp knock on my office door made me jump. My head smacked against the hanging overhead lamp and I cursed under my breath. Things were crazy since the Horsemen had shown up, and Bandit wasn't with me today, making me instinctively edgy. I set aside the drawing I was working on and called, "Come in."

A wave of green hair fell through my office door as Moira pushed past it and closed the door behind her. Her dark green eyes scanned me, her forest colored brows drawn together in what appeared to be worry, but I couldn't feel it. My empath gifts only extended so far, and while I could usually guess when Bandit got up in arms about something, Moira was more complicated than that.

"Something wrong?" I asked, motioning to the chair in front of my desk. She ignored my offer and walked around to my side. Pushing the papers into a pile, she slid back onto my desk, letting her legs dangle a few inches from the ground.

"I'm worried about you."

"Okay," I drawled out, taking a loose breath. "Is this about the Horsemen?"

"Possibly," Moira said, biting her lip. She glanced at me, looking up and down like she was searching for something. I was the same Ruby I've always been: ripped up jeans and unbrushed hair, pulled back to hide my general laziness. "I just feel like there's something you're not telling me. Did something happen with them?"

I let out a sigh, considering my answer. Apart from last Friday, when Laran took me to a bar that gave me some kind of demonic high, not much had happened. Sure, the guys were still following me everywhere, showing up at the oddest of times, but I was beginning to settle into a routine with it. Typically, Rysten came first, then Laran, followed by Allistair. I'd only seen Julian a handful of times; unlike the other three, who were giving me subtly stronger fuck-me-vibes with every day that passed. I wasn't sure how much of their spending time with me was for my actual protection, and how much was them attempting to sink their claws into me.

Moira coughed, and I blinked once. *Shit.*

"So," she said with narrowed eyes, "there is something that happened, isn't there?"

I leaned back in my chair and kicked my feet up beside her on the thick glass surface. I tilted my head back in my chair, relaxing my spine as I stared up at the ceiling, counting the flecks of dust.

"Not something specific, per se. It's just been a long few days."

"The Horsemen are getting possessive."

Well that wasn't what I expected to come out of her mouth. She hadn't been around us all that much, and I hadn't mentioned it. I cracked my knuckles absentmindedly while I asked, "What makes you say that?"

I couldn't see her face, but I suspected she was giving me a look along the lines of *are you kidding me?* She huffed under her breath and I smirked just a little, waiting for her answer.

"Josh came by the house before you got home yesterday, as per his usual Sunday groveling routine. I tried to chase him off, but Laran showed up. I think Josh just about shit bricks when Laran told him that you're theirs and he'll feed him to the hounds of Hell if he comes near you again."

I facepalmed as I let out a heavy sigh. *Feed him to Hell hounds? Very creative.*

"Well, that sounds unpleasant," I said lamely. Moira didn't reply. I raised my head from the back of my chair to see her watching me. She was not amused.

"They've taken a liking to you, Ruby."

"You don't know that for certain..." My words fell short when she gave me the look. The Moira look. She wasn't buying it. I let out the most unflattering of noises, somewhere between a sigh and a groan, as I slouched back into my chair.

"Yes, I do."

"Admitting it doesn't change anything. It just makes the current situation even more messed up," I muttered, throwing an arm over my eyes.

"Maybe it's just because they think they need to protect you; maybe it's more. On the bright side, if it is a passing obsession, they should get over it eventually—" She stopped mid-sentence and examined me carefully. "I'm not helping, am I?"

I didn't want to be rude. It wasn't her fault her own anxiety was leaking over into me and made my slightly cautious brain light up like a police siren telling me I should run like hell. I'd been taking on others' emotions long enough, I knew how to tell the difference between what I was feeling and what they unintentionally pushed on me. With Moira, it just seemed that I was more in tune and struggled on where to draw the line.

"Not really. I know you mean well, but the best I can do is to just roll with it for now. It's not like I have a lot of choice in getting them to leave me alone. Besides," I said, placing a gentle hand on her knee, "they really aren't that bad. Julian is a bit standoffish, and Allistair likes to push my buttons. Laran's pretty cool when he's not being all 'War smash', and Rysten is—" Her soft smile went sour and she swatted my hand away.

"Don't do that! You know I don't like it when you mess with my emotions. It's weird," she said. I raised an eyebrow. "It's weird if I try to help you feel better, but it's not weird when you make people's eardrums explode?" I asked, fighting a grin. She nodded without a trace of humor. "Whatever." I rolled my eyes and stood to gather my things.

"I actually came to tell you Rysten's here. I just wanted to talk with you before you left. You can tell him, and the rest of his cohort, that I'm taking you out this Friday, and no, they're not invited." I slung my bag over my shoulder and grabbed my keys.

"It's my birthday. Shouldn't I be the one that says who's invited?" I asked absentmindedly. I already knew the answer. It was Moira I was talking to, and normal people logic wouldn't work here. She was just as possessive as the Horsemen and didn't give a single fuck.

"Nope, they've been hogging you since they showed up, and you only turn twenty-three once. I've made plans for us. They can find someone else to stalk for the night," she said as she hopped off my desk and opened the door. I followed her out into the lobby where Rysten was standing off to the side, both eyebrows raised as he watched us approach.

"It took you that long to tell her I'm here?"

She bristled instantly, and he grinned like a fool. Out of all the Horsemen, he was the only one that truly seemed to take pleasure in tormenting her. Not that she was all that innocent either.

"It makes sense that you're Pestilence. You're more of a pest than the other three," Moira responded icily. It wasn't even very funny, but the venom with which she said it made Rysten let out a dark chuckle.

"I've heard that one a time or two. You might want to get some new jokes, banshee," he said holding his hand out for me. I ignored the invitation and proceeded towards the door.

"I'll see you tonight," I called over my shoulder without waiting for a reply. The chill in the autumn air hit me full force and swept the strands of my messy bun away from my face. The sky was a dull shade of black that matched the city cement, but the wind howled as it sent dead leaves tunneling down the alleys of Portland.

"What's on the evening agenda today, love?" Rysten asked, strolling up beside me, his footsteps silent as the grave.

"I'm tired. I think I'm going to go home and watch *How to Get Away with Murder* with Bandit," I said.

Rysten frowned. "You're a demon. I don't think it's that difficult figuring out how to get away with murder, but if you need someone taken care of, I can do it for you..." His voice started to trail off as I let out the first true laugh I'd had this past week. I had to put a hand against my car to steady myself as water pricked my eyes.

"I don't need someone killed, Rysten." I said hoarsely.

"But you said—"

"It's a TV show about these law students that—" I stopped at the first hint of a smirk on his lips. He leaned forward and whispered, "Gotcha."

I groaned under my breath and opened the driver's side door. That dickwad. He knew exactly what I was talking about. I slammed the door and started the engine, taking my foot off the brake right as the passenger side door opened and Rysten got in beside me.

"Don't be mad, love. You said you were tired. I thought you could use a laugh," he coaxed me, batting his eyelashes.

"Uh huh," I grumbled under my breath. The words were sweet as sugar, but I didn't believe the sincerity I heard there.

"I'll have you know that Viola Davis is one of my favorite actresses," he continued. I rolled my eyes as I pulled out onto the main street.

"How do you even know who she is? I thought you

spent all your time in Hell until Lucifer"— I searched for an adequate word that didn't sound dickish, given that they thought he was my father. They'd guarded him for thousands of years, and I had no idea how their relationship had been with the King of Hell—"uh...died. I mean, isn't that your entire job?"

Rysten went quiet for a moment, and I thought he wasn't going to answer. "While we did serve in guarding him, he was not who we were created for. When you came along, it was like we finally saw the purpose for our existence. We were supposed to stay in Hell so that no one knew Lola smuggled you out, but instead, we ended up taking turns coming to earth. We didn't know where you were, and we weren't supposed to look until the time came. Being here on earth, though, we were closer to you than in Hell—" He stopped abruptly, like he'd said more than he intended.

My knuckles turned white against the red fur that lined the steering wheel.

Bit by bit, the pieces were falling into place about the Horsemen, and while I didn't know where attraction played into all of this, I was pretty sure I just figured out the possessiveness. If they were created for Lucifer's daughter, whoever she is, it made sense for them to feel so attached.

"So, you spent your time here watching TV, and that's how you discovered Viola?" I turned the subject right back to what we were supposed to be making small talk about. I didn't want to think about the real heir of Hell, or ruin Rysten's mood by pointing out for the hundredth time that I'm not her.

"Yeah, sometimes. I spent a lot of time going to concerts around the world, meeting people, learning about humans. I knew that you'd be raised like one, and the others were too daft to think that when this happened, it might be scary for you. I wanted to be the one you got close to." He smiled a little, not quite his brazen confidence I was getting used to, but something more genuine. We didn't say anything else for the rest of the drive home.

As I killed the engine, I couldn't help the words from popping out of my mouth. "You want to come inside and watch TV with me?"

Rysten grinned. "You sure the green one will be okay with that?"

"Moira will live. She's already staked her claim on Friday night. We're going out and she said none of you are invited," I replied, throwing my door open. I was pleasantly surprised that Josh wasn't waiting on my driveway when I got home. Maybe Laran really did scare the shit out of him. The thought brought me an obscene amount of glee.

"I can't say I'm terribly surprised. She heard me on the phone with Laran before she went back to get you. He wanted us to take you out for your birthday," Rysten sighed. I thought back to Moira's adamant insistence. Yeah, she was sneaky enough to pull that. Not that I was shocked or upset about it. For the most part, I only saw one or two Horsemen at a time. The four of them together were overwhelming, and I was more than happy to avoid that a bit longer.

I trudged up to the front door and Bandit peeked his

head through the blinds. I smiled as I swung the door open and got mauled with his hugs. He jumped from the corner of the couch onto my chest, wrapping his arms around my neck.

"I missed you, too," I murmured, flicking the light on. I tossed my bag on one of the couches and carried him into the kitchen. Pulling out a Tupperware of cooked chicken, I proceeded to heat it in the microwave and feed Bandit his dinner.

While he was eating, I excused myself back to my room and changed into yoga pants. As I pulled the dark red sweater over my head, I noticed something strange in the mirror. Between my breasts were two little black dots. I moved closer, running my fingers over them. They weren't large or bumpy, but they were placed in a straight line. I frowned.

What the hell is it?

A sharp knock on my bedroom door startled me. "You okay, Ruby?"

I rolled my eyes, already somewhat regretting inviting him inside. I dropped my sweater and turned away from the mirror. I'd deal with it later when I didn't have prying eyes watching my every move. I slipped into the hallway and closed my bedroom door behind me, not realizing how close Rysten was until a breath of warm air brushed the back of my neck. My skin broke out in goosebumps. I spun around, trying to keep a modicum of distance between us, but it was hopeless in the narrow hallway.

Rysten's dark green eyes stared down at me. Intense and mischievous. My mouth went dry and I swallowed hard.

"See something you like?" he rumbled. There was a challenge in his voice that had me imagining how soft his hair would feel tousled in my fingers, his head... I blinked, pushing the thoughts aside.

"Yep"— my eyes slid right past him just as he began to grin—"my couch."

Rysten clutched his chest. "You wound me."

I snorted and squeezed by him, holding my breath so I didn't inhale his scent. It was unlikely he'd smell like post-gym body odor, because that would be way too convenient, wouldn't it? I settled in the corner of my oversized sectional couch, the grey microsuede upholstery welcoming me to lean back. I stretched across the couch for the remote, and Rysten sat cozy, flush against me. Of course. Out of all the spaces he could sit, he would pick the only one that is literally right next to me.

I didn't say anything as I pulled up the TV guide and turned on the fifth episode of season one, but just as I leaned back, Rysten put his arm across the back of the couch. I glanced sideways out of the corner of my eye, and the devilish grin I found on his face made me bite my cheek.

I crossed my arms over my chest as the show started. My thick sweater made it so we weren't touching, but a pleasant warmth radiated from him. Unlike Allistair's presence, that caused a scorching heat and spurned a need in me, Rysten's was a comfortable steadiness that made me ache. It was delicious and frustrating at the same time.

After forty-five minutes of sitting still as a rock, I shifted to try to get more comfortable—and farther away.

Rysten chose that moment to scoot even closer, pinning me between him and the couch as I sat crisscrossed beside him.

I bit my lip hard and gasped when I tasted blood. The tangy scent of ichor and something else caught me off guard.

"You alright?" Rysten asked. I turned my head a fraction of the way towards him and nodded, not trusting my mouth to work.

"You're bleeding." His eyes dropped to my lower lip as I freed it from my teeth. He raised his other hand and ran the pad of his thumb across my lower lip. A burning started in my chest, hot and scorching, as it spread throughout my limbs. Adrenaline spiked my system as he drew his hand away, a single drop of dark blue blood staining it. He brought his thumb to his lips, and his tongue flicked out, licking the single drop away.

I don't know why the hell that turned me on so much. Maybe it wasn't the act. Maybe it was the look in his eyes; the way he watched me while he did it.

Frozen in my spot, I could do little more than watch as he reached out again and ran his thumb across my lower lip. I found myself leaning into him as he slid his cool fingers along my jaw.

I shivered as his warm breath hit the sensitive part of my ear. His lips brushed against me, barely making contact, as he whispered, "Tell me when to stop."

Heat pooled low in my stomach, but my brain didn't seem to be working. I unraveled beneath the curve of his lips as he trailed them down my jaw. The last thing I saw as my eyes fell closed was his expression: hungry, but vulnerable. A moment passed, suspended there as our breath mingled. That scent that I couldn't define filled the air around me; intoxicating as I breathed it in.

It was wrong. I knew it was wrong, because nothing this good was ever right. It was rare that I found someone who so fully captured my attention as he and the Horsemen did. I was a damn fool for caving, and I almost pulled away. Until he said, "You're everything I didn't know I wanted."

His lips met mine, smooth and sweet, but the gentleness didn't stay for long. He shifted his arm from the back of the couch to wrap around me as I uncrossed my legs and turned into him. His fingers tangled into my hair, cupping the back of my head, pulling me closer as his tongue parted the seam of my lips. Coaxing me. Claiming me. I reached out, fisting his shirt, pulling him closer than I'd dared to with anyone in such a long time, the other night notwithstanding. That was because I was high. This was exhilarating and frightening, but the air crackled with a tension that couldn't be denied.

I kissed him like my life depended on it, but that was nothing compared to the way his lips destroyed me. Fuck living. He kissed me like he was dying. Like this was the first and last kiss we'd ever have—and maybe it was. But he was doing an awfully good job at branding it into my memory.

He broke the kiss just when I realized I needed air or I'd faint, but his lips didn't leave me. He kissed his way back up my jaw, and left stinging bites all down my neck. I arched into the little dose of pain, silently urging him on. Pushing him to give me more. He pulled the crook of my sweater to the side, exposing my shoulder so that he could taste every inch of me. He left a string of reddened skin, slight purple teeth marks to the very edge of my shoulder before making his way back. A low moan escaped my lips as his teeth scraped the sensitive part of my neck, just beneath my ear.

His hands moved to my hips as I straddled his lap and ground myself into the hard bulge beneath me. The breath hissed between his lips, and he bit down on my earlobe.

"What do you want?" he asked. My hands seemed to move on their own accord as they slipped beneath the edge of his shirt. He bit my earlobe again, a touch more pressure. I let out another breathy moan as he said, "What. Do. You. Want? Tell me. Soon enough, I won't be able to stop."

His breath was cold against my burning skin.

I scrambled to get off his lap as fast as I could, but he didn't let go.

"Let go of me," I said. I bit the inside of my cheek to stop from moaning as his hand slipped underneath my shirt. The circles he drew against my lower back with his thumb sent an inferno blazing through my self-control, but I held strong.

"Why?" he murmured, leaning into me.

"Because we can't do this."

"Give me one reason why, and I'll let you go," he whispered, his face against my neck, his words against my skin. I'd avoided this conversation for the last week, and again at the diner when Allistair confronted me. Trapped with Rysten between my legs, I had to speak up now, or whatever happened next was on me.

"Tell me *why* you want me," I said. Rysten ran his lips along the edge of my collarbone, and his non-answer was point enough. "You don't even know, do you? That's the problem. You have no choice *but* to want me, and I can't screw someone who has no choice in the matter."

Rysten froze beneath me, but did not release his hold. I became painfully aware of the slow, steady thrum of my own heartbeat as it reverberated beneath my skin. Rysten slowly pulled back.

"Ruby, have you been torturing yourself this entire time thinking that we could only possibly want you because we have no choice?" he asked, a smile playing on the corners of his lips. I didn't find this funny in the slightest.

"I've never met a man where that's not the case," I replied tersely. He slipped his entire hand underneath my sweater and flattened it against my back.

"We've already had this conversation before. I'm not a man."

"Man. Demon. You are still male. You're all the same where I'm concerned. I've had women come onto me before, so it's not gender specific, really. My point is that if I sleep with you, it won't be your choice, and that's kind of rapey, if you ask me."

Rysten didn't hold back from laughing at me. I pushed his chest trying to wiggle my way off him, but he wasn't letting up any more than he was before. His laugh trailed off into a heavy silence, the air between us stretched taut with pressure.

"Ruby, love, I can't believe we're having this conversation right now, but if we need to have it for you to feel comfortable, then we'll have it. I want *you*. And not because it's my job, or because you're a succubus. You think I can't see past the draw of a succubus? That the allure captures me and renders me unable to make my own decisions? Yes, I want you because the very smell of your skin makes me hard. Every time you bite your lip, I imagine what you taste like; what it feels like to bite that very same lip and hear you moan. But those are not the reasons *why*. Those are simply *wants*." He paused, letting out a strained breath. "You have a fire in you that I have not seen in anyone in a very long time. A wildness about you. I told you once already: you are not what I thought you'd be. But now that I know you, I don't know how I could possibly imagine you any different. You are everything that we could have ever wanted you to be, and so much more. When I am with you, I realize how lucky we are that no one ever swept you off your feet, because I don't think that any of us would have let them live if they had."

My mouth popped open. I didn't know what to say to that. His eyes were dark and lustful, but he didn't seem to have the crazed obsession I was used to seeing. He'd be fumbling a lot more if he did, and he sure as hell couldn't string his thoughts together so well.

"How do you know you're not being affected without realizing it?" I asked.

"You do realize who you're talking to? You know what I am. I'd make for a poor Horsemen if I didn't have the knowledge or strength to fight off desire. And not even you, Hell's heir, are strong enough to make me do anything against my will. That's why we were created: to be the only equals that could protect and balance you."

Aside for the being Hell's heir part, he had a point. The legends never told what *kind* of demons they were, only what you would find if you ever crossed them. I couldn't argue his logic that my few latent powers weren't nearly enough to force his hand.

Then the door opened. And Moira walked in. Her eyes wavered between Rysten and me, and she let out a dramatic sigh.

"I see why you're beginning to think they're not so bad," she commented. My face burned as a blush crept across my cheeks. I scrambled back, and this time Rysten let me go. Moira cocked an eyebrow and nodded towards him. "Time to go, pest," she said unapologetically.

Rysten didn't argue. He simply stood and said, "I'll see you tomorrow, Ruby. Get some rest."

I watched him disappear outside my front door and I turned towards a rather pissed off Moira. She didn't say anything as she walked back to her room. Her silence spoke louder than any words she could have chosen.

CHAPTER 12

Four days had passed, and Moira hadn't said shit. The morning after she saw me with Rysten, I had woken up to her continuing on like everything was normal. Except it wasn't. In the time since, not once had she bitched about the Horsemen. Hadn't engaged in her usual antics with Rysten. She was acting normal...but that wasn't 'normal Moira,' and it was driving me fucking nuts. At least our plans were still on for tonight. I closed shop early in the hopes of trying to talk with her without the Horsemen showing up, but she was particularly good at avoiding me when she wanted to.

Standing in the shower, I glowered into the plume of steam that wrapped around me. The water was turned up as hot as I could get it, and it still wasn't hot enough. Flipping the nozzle off, I used the other hand to wring my hair out. Strands of wet, dark hair clung to my fingers, reflecting indigo in the light.

The bathroom door thudded twice as Moira called

out, "We need to leave in half an hour if we're going to make it there before the switch."

The switch? I frowned, wrapping the purple towel around me. She made it sound like we were going to a prison. I crossed the cold tile floors, slick with condensation. The door knob was slippery in my grasp as I turned the handle and asked, "What do you mean 'make it there before the switch'?"

Moira smiled, and I saw a little bit of the stunning banshee underneath the glittering pale eyeshadow. "You'll just have to see, now won't you?" she said, turning on her heel. The black baby doll dress she wore swished just past her ass, her legs barely protected by black floral tights. Her mint colored skin practically glowed beneath the sheer fabric. It's such a shame the humans couldn't see her in her full glory. She would be wearing a glamor tonight, just as she always did, and that beautiful green would disappear.

At least we weren't prison crashing. Not even Moira would get all dressed up for that. Looks like we were going partying at an unknown indoor location, given that it wasn't even thirty degrees outside and she liked the cold about as much as I did.

I closed the bathroom door and got to work on my hair, blow drying it into soft billowing waves that really showed off the stunning blues. I applied only the bare essentials in makeup and moved on to my outfit when Moira came back in.

"Why are you still wearing a bathrobe?" She swung open my closet door without waiting for a reply. It took less than a minute before she was ripping things off the hangers and tossing them at me. "Put these on. We gotta go."

I disrobed and dressed in the skinny jeans and the crop top she gave me, making a mental note to grab a jacket before we left. Moira grabbed my shoulders and turned me towards the metal framed mirror. A branch of iron thorns surrounded my scantily clad body. Moira had chosen well; the crop showed off my curves while still flattering my tall frame.

"I think you should—"

I zoned out as something caught my eye. The number of dots seated on my sternum had increased. Previously, there were two sitting across from each other. There was now a third that sat an inch lower on the right side.

"Ruby, are you even listening to me?" she snapped, pulling me from my thoughts.

"Yeah," I said, rubbing my chest where the dots were.

"Excellent," she said gleefully, smacking her nude lips together, a pair of spiked black heels in her hand. I took one look at the shoes and groaned. "What are you waiting for? Hurry up!"

I could do little more than comply. At least she was acting like herself.

Within the next two minutes, we were out the door and on our way, hooker heels and all. Bandit kept grabbing at my leg wanting to come with, but I knew he wouldn't be welcome in whatever public shindig Moira planned on taking us to. In the end, all it took was can of sardines and he was content to let me go.

Fifteen minutes later, and almost two car accidents, thanks to Moira's driving, we pulled up outside Pandora's

Box, the hottest and most exclusive nightclub in town. I'd only ever heard rumors about what went on inside, usually from my clients. How Moira was going to pull this one off was beyond me.

Outside, the club was sleek and void of any windows or doors, apart from the front entrance that currently had a line wrapped around the block. Moira pulled up to the curb, and the valet that approached us gave her a questioning purse of his lips.

She hopped out of the car and handed him the keys, ignoring his mutterings about how he wasn't sure if we were in the right place. I couldn't blame him. Her ten-year old Camry didn't really fit the bill with one taillight out and a dent on the front bumper. True to form, Moira didn't give two shits. She passed him a fifty and said, "Keep the change."

The valet, pleased with his tip, changed his attitude as I clambered out of the car. With the damn heels, I was well over six feet tall. Moira was wearing some impressive shoes as well, and that made our height difference almost minimal. I glanced between her and the line, because I didn't know about her feet, but mine were not going to put up with standing in line for three hours just to be turned away at the door.

As if she'd read my mind, Moira linked our arms and leaned in. "Relax. I have connections," she muttered as she led us up to the front of the line. A bouncer took one look at us, and just when I thought he was going to turn us away, his face lit up in a warm smile.

"Hey, Moira, this the friend you were telling me about?"

Moira nodded demurely, but even in the low light coming from the sign above, I could see a faint blush creep across her cheeks. Bouncer boy flashed his dimples again and unclipped the rope, ushering us through.

We hadn't even crossed the threshold when I leaned in to ask, "So, what did you have to do to pull this off?"

Moira's smile only increased as we took our first steps into the dazzling lights that were Pandora's Box. "You don't want to know," she said and smirked at me. She's right; I didn't.

Still linked arm in arm, we walked toward the bar. Purple and blue lights danced across the crowd of bodies on a dance floor that was packed so tight, I didn't think even Moira could slip between them. Rhythmic dance music pulsed through the air, the vibrations thrumming against my skin, luring me with its hypnotic melody.

The bartender turned towards us, his gold bow-tie shimmering in the light. Moira flashed him a come-hither look as she crooked her finger and beckoned him closer. I rolled my eyes as he asked, "What can I get for you ladies?"

"Dirty martini," Moira rattled off, looking over at me expectantly.

An odd feeling crept through my veins. I couldn't place what caused it, but I didn't like it.

"Ruby! What drink?"

"I'm not sure..." I muttered. I took a quick glance around the room, but there wasn't a demon in sight. We'd been out drinking hundreds of times, and nothing ever happened. So why was I feeling paranoid suddenly?

Because drugs and an imp with grabby hands in the middle of butt-fuck nowhere...

"It's your birthday," she said crossly. "I did not suck tha—"

"Birthday girl, eh?" the bartender said, cutting her off mid-rant. He gave me a lopsided smile and said, "I've got something for you. On the house."

"Alright," I agreed. Moira and I settled in at the bar and I took another sweeping glance of the club. There was just so much to look at: the dancers, the lounge, the winding staircase that led up to darkened hallways with unmarked doors, hiding secrets of their own. All bathed in shifting violet light.

"What do you think's up there?" I asked her.

"No clue." She shrugged, turning back to the counter as the bartender came with our drinks. Moira took a sip of her martini and let out a little sigh of happiness while I stared at the swirling concoction before me. It was pale white with just the faintest hint of blue whorls. I took a daring sip.

"Oh," I murmured, blinking. It was good! Really good. It reminded me of a piña-colada, but somehow tangy and less sweet.

"You like it?" she asked. I nodded as a steady warmth built in my chest. I felt lighter, but not out-of-my-mind-sexed-up like I was at the demon bar. I finished my drink within minutes and ordered another.

"Ruby?" I turned in my seat, just as someone put their hand on the small my back. I knew that voice, and it definitely didn't belong in a club with me.

"Josh?" The steady buzz building inside me made my lips loose. "How'd you get in here?"

"I know a guy," he said smugly. His hand still hadn't moved. He was getting cozy as he placed himself between me and the empty barstool. I frowned.

"Stop touching me," I said. The bartender chose that moment to appear with my drink and I smiled gratefully. Josh dropped his hand from my back, but didn't move away from me otherwise.

"I just—I need to talk to you, Ruby. Me and you, without your...bodyguards."

I took a long sip of my drink. *Bodyguards...that sounds about right.*

"Josh"— my voice was obnoxiously loud, even by my standards—"how many times do I have to tell you that—"

"You don't get it, Ruby!"

I swallowed hard, considering his once bright blue eyes, now bloodshot...but there was something else there. It didn't look human. *What is wrong with him?*

"I can't stop thinking about you. I know you're having a hard time forgiving me, but please hear me out," he pleaded. I took another swig of my drink, prepared to cut all pretenses of civility from my voice.

"Leave. Her. Alone," Moira said in a voice like death. "Stop following her. Stop showing up at our house to talk to her. If I see you come around one more time, I'm getting Rysten to come take care of your ass and make you disappear. You hear me, Josh? Go. Away." Moira jumped to my defense with a fierceness I couldn't have predicted, and what's more, she even brought Rysten into it. I turned to my best friend, temporarily stunned, but her glowing green eyes were focused on Josh.

"You just don't get it!" he said, louder than before. "I can't eat! I can't sleep! I can't think about anything but Ruby!"

Devil fucking take him already. This was getting old.

His obsession was getting worse, and I wasn't even around him enough to fuel it. Without warning, he placed another hand on my back, rubbing it in fevered, rhythmic circles. His need to touch me, to be *with* me, was getting out of control. I swung around in my chair and bared my teeth, the little bit of power I did have rose to the surface and made my hair crackle.

"Don't fucking touch me. You're crazy. Obsessed. And you know what? You and Kendall deserve each other." Any normal person would have let me go by now, but he wasn't normal anymore. This wasn't normal. He was close enough to me that I could feel the hard on in his pants, and the way it twitched every time I spoke told me all I needed to know.

This is why succubi cut and run.

Humans were weak. I hadn't even slept with him. Yet, he was just as crazy as the one I did sleep with at sixteen. The very memory made me shiver, but the fear turned to anger as more heat flooded my system.

Moira placed a hand on my shoulder, forcing me to swivel back towards her. She grabbed both shoulders and looked me in the eye.

"He's not worth it, Ruby. We've been down this road before," she said quietly. It was the subtlest of words that she could use to talk about what happened nearly seven years ago. "It's your birthday, and I won't let this loser ruin it. Okay?"

I nodded, and behind me, Josh let out the coldest, most deranged of laughs. In a club that was bursting with music and bodies, it was lost on all but us.

"You're mine, Ruby." That was the last thing he said before I felt his angry presence disappear in the crowd. Moira's mouth was pressed in a thin line, but we both ignored him until he was gone.

"Thank you," I whispered.

"For what?" she asked, tilting her head.

"For always being there."

She eased her grip on my shoulders and slid her arms around me. "I'll always be here. Even when you don't tell me things," she murmured into my shoulder. A shred of guilt ran through me as I hazily recalled the last few days.

"I'm sorry about that. I'm just...confused when it comes to them. I don't even know how I feel about it myself—"

"I'm not getting after you, Ruby. You're allowed to keep things to yourself, but I worry about you because of shit like Josh happening. The Horsemen don't seem like that. I trust you know what you're getting yourself into. Just let me know before I try to cock block someone and blow out their eardrums, eh?" I must not be the only one that was feeling the burn, because Moira was starting to slur her words a little.

"You're drunk. The Moira I know never forgives this easily."

Moira pulled away, a demonic glint in her eye. "It's your birthday. Call this an exception. I'm not nearly drunk enough, and neither are you. Finish that," she motioned to the half-full mystery drink. "Hey, bartender! Bring us some shots for the birthday girl!"

I tipped back the remainder of the cloudy sweetness.

Bottoms up.

CHAPTER 13

We only made it through two rounds of shots before we went stumbling drunk onto the dance floor. Devil knows how I made it in the heels I was wearing, but I did. The techno beat of the music kept me going as one song blended into the other. Around me, the room seemed to be gaining more energy as the club continued to fill with people. The lights dropped into a darker hue as the music became louder.

"I'll be right back!" I yelled to Moira.

She turned her head fractionally and shouted, "What?"

"Bathroom," I said back, trying to mouth the word so she could read my lips.

"Need me to come with you?" she mouthed in return, laughing and pointing to herself and then to me.

I shook my head no, waving her off as I began weaving through the crowd. The surrounding people pushed and pulled, swaying with the music like one living thing. I stumbled off the dance floor and caught myself on the stair railing that led to the next level.

The bouncer next to it smiled at me. He was the same one from outside, but it was only then that I realized I recognized him from somewhere.

"Have we met before?" I asked. He said something, but I couldn't hear his response. The words came out distorted. They didn't blend with the music; they warped around it. I needed to find the bathroom. Maybe some cold water would help me. It was difficult to communicate that I needed the toilets, but he seemed to know what I was asking.

He pointed upstairs and said, "Your boyfriend's up there waiting for you."

I must have heard that wrong. I didn't have a boyfriend. Maybe he said bathroom?

He unclipped the rope and ushered me through. I was halfway up the stairs when I started to get dizzy. A sudden need to lie down hit me and gripping the rail was the only thing that kept me upright. I eased my way up the rest of the stairs and stumbled down the hallway.

My legs didn't want to cooperate. I lost my footing and fell towards a door. Strong arms caught me, pulling me back.

"Thank you," I slurred. One of the hands that caught me reached forward and opened the door. I stumbled in, my eyes having trouble adjusting to the low light. Hot breath fanned my skin as someone's lips began trailing down my neck.

Behind me the door gave a harsh audible click.

"Wha—" I started to protest, but the world tilted as

the stranger pushed me onto something flat and hard. My face smacked into the surface and sent pain shooting through me. Sharp and cruel. I whimpered as the stranger started turning my body over, my back against the cold surface beneath.

Even in the dim light with inebriation setting in, I recognized the man pulling my legs apart.

"J-joshhh...wh-why are—"

"You wouldn't listen to me, Ruby," he said harshly. His voice sounded far away as my consciousness began to retreat. I wanted to move my legs to kick him, but I no longer had control. My entire body had gone numb.

"This is your fault. You think I want to do this?" My legs hanging limp over the edge, he placed himself between them. His hands wrapped around the back of my thighs, pulling me closer. I wanted to scream, but I couldn't form words anymore. I couldn't do anything.

"I can't get you out of my mind, but you won't come back to me. I hurt for you so much, Ruby. Not even Kendall can soothe it anymore. It must be you." He continued speaking, muttering to himself. A blind panic set into me. I knew what was about to go down, but I couldn't put the words to it. I couldn't stop it.

Josh's hands continued groping me, reaching beneath my top. His sweaty palms wrapped around my breasts, and terror seized me. He was seriously going to do this.

"You wouldn't let me touch these when we were together. You were such a prude. Not anymore, though, are you, Ruby?" Squeezing my breasts, his face in my neck, I could feel his pathetic excuse for a cock pushing against me. Pins and needles prickled my skin as I tried to cry out for someone. Anyone. I screamed and screamed, but I was locked in a nightmare where no one could hear me.

Josh's fumbling movements worsened the more he touched me. My skin did that to people. I was such a fool for even wanting someone to pass the time with. I was lonely and starving. For attention. For sex. For everything. I was a fucking demon deprived of all that I needed, so I played with fire and now I was going to burn.

Burn.

I was burning inside.

"You're mine, and I will have you." Josh pulled back, fumbling to undo his pants. I couldn't see the movements, I couldn't move my head, but I could hear every notch of his zipper, and every rustle of clothing as his pants dropped to the floor.

It was so similar to before. It was scary.

Except this time, I didn't have Moira to save me.

Josh's filthy hands wrapped around my waist, pulling me closer as he rubbed himself against me. It was savage and disgusting. His hands clumsily tugged at my shirt, pulling it off, my head lolling as he jerked the fabric over and tossed it aside. I could feel everything and nothing, and I couldn't escape. I was no longer me. My consciousness retreated further, searching for safety in some dark corner of my mind.

The girl on the table was pinned and helpless, but not so far away—I was burning with hatred. Burning like I never had before.

As his mouth wrapped around my nipple, I stopped screaming for help, and started screaming for death.

His death.

I wanted him to bleed for this.

I was going to hurt him.

Hell, when I came to, I was going to kill him.

It was that simple thought that unlocked something inside of me. Something I'd never known was there. For the first time, lying on a table, drugged and unable to move, I saw a glimpse of something...not of this world.

Something dark.

Deadly.

And as his hands unbuttoned my pants, that something cracked its eye open.

RYSTEN

Something reached into my chest and yanked my heart out.

At least that's what it felt like.

Out of nowhere, a pure undiluted terror seized me. It demanded my attention; all of it, as the searing pain crawled inside me. I grasped at my chest as I fell back into the sofa. My wine slipped from my hand, spilling across the pale furniture, staining it a deep burgundy. The pain eased for a moment, and I looked up around the room. Julian gripped the island counter hard enough that the quartz crumbled beneath his fingers.

"What the fuck was that?" Laran yelled down the hallway. He emerged holding a hand to his chest, his eyes glowing red.

"I have no idea, but I'm going to assume we all felt the same thing?" Julian replied tersely. The words were hardly out of his mouth when it started again. Worse than it was before. The pain that ripped through me burned.

Only when the scorching heat died down, did my vision clear enough to see the world around me.

Laran's knees must have buckled, because he'd fallen to the floor. Allistair was collapsed sideways into the wall, his glass of scotch seeping onto the carpet in an amber pool. Even my brother, the strongest of us Horsemen, was leaning onto the counter for support. A vein in his temple bulged; the only indication Death would ever give he was in pain.

"Who could possibly attack all four of us?" I breathed.

Silence enveloped us as another wave of heat tore through my chest. This surge tasted of fury, not just pain. The psychic power bypassed my shields like they were nothing, igniting a torture I had never known.

As it waned, I realized a small piece of the essence was familiar. It was wild...

The truth and the horror hit me at once.

"Ruby."

All it took was her name to spur us into action.

I had no idea how she'd done it. How she could possibly be hiding so much power? Allistair had said he felt it...but in that moment, I didn't care. All I cared about was finding her and ending whoever was hurting her—if there was even anything left of them.

We were the Horsemen, and we were immortal. She had brought the four strongest beings that roamed any world, outside of herself, to their knees. It was very plausible that whoever hurt her was already dead.

"We need to find her now," Laran said.

I shadow walked out of the room and onto the streets

of Portland. They would catch up if they hadn't already. Right now, Ruby was the most important thing. I made it three steps down the street, before another wave of uncontainable rage washed through me. It was crippling, and I stumbled, but I would not stop. I would not fail her.

I used the pain and the rage and the terror to fuel my hunt. They would lead me to her.

I had no idea where she was, or how to reach her, but somehow, her power guided me.

Like a string connecting the two of us, it wrapped around me, pulling me towards ground zero.

I came around another corner and stopped immediately at a door. I could feel it in my bones. She was here. This was it. I was standing at a club called Pandora's Box.

I pushed through the line of people to the front, punching the guard that dared block my way. They were not my concern. Inside, it smelled of liquor and sweat. The humans danced, if you could call it that, grinding on one another in sync with the music.

The lights above shifted and moved as I dove into the crowd, pushing the humans out of the way as I went. I ripped through the dance floor and scanned the bar. Ruby wasn't here, but I could feel her close. Her pain was more pronounced now. Her terror more defined.

Images flashed through my mind.

My blood ran cold.

Lured by the invisible line, I found myself at the base of the stairs. Not a single bouncer tried to stop me. They were more preoccupied with the humans that had started collapsing one by one. Ruby's power tainted the air, and I had no doubt she was the cause.

RYSTEN

I raced up the stairs after War and Death; Famine at my heels. The world slowed down to one single purpose, and that was getting to Ruby. I was so focused on reaching her, that when Julian kicked the door open, I was unprepared for the rage that took me as I stared at the bare ass of her ex as he was removing the jeans from her limp legs.

He'd drugged her. He'd molested her. Now he was about to rape her.

I lost all sense of rational and let my fury consume him.

CHAPTER 14

The door burst open and light danced across the ceiling.

Josh halted in his fevered attempt at removing my pants, and the brief interruption ripped my consciousness away from the inner beast. But the damage was done. I now knew she was there, deep inside of me. Sleeping in a cage, waiting for the door to open. My vision swam as voices began to file in.

My head had cleared enough I could make them out.

"I told you what would happen if you came near her again." Fire blazed to life overhead, and a face appeared before me.

Dark sage eyes and white blonde hair. Julian's hard profile stared down at me. His expression unreadable. He reached a hand out, his fingertips barely touching my forehead as he brushed my hair aside.

An icy wave ran through me. Cold. Brutal. It was the kind of cold that hurt so much it blistered. Every inch of my skin prickled against his touch, absorbing unspeakable pain. When it finally started to ebb, I found myself clinging to it and wanting more.

"Can you hear me, Ruby?" he asked softly.

I tried to nod my head, and to my surprise, it actually moved. I swallowed hard, tears pricking my eyes. "Y-yes," I rasped.

Slowly, but surely, the numbness began fading from my body as I came to. Enough so that I could make out Josh's screaming.

I struggled to sit up, and Julian put a hand out to hold me down.

"You don't want to see this."

"...have to," I whispered.

Something unspoken passed between us. Maybe it was the moment. Maybe it was the remnants of whatever drugs Josh gave me. I don't know, but in that moment, Julian understood me as my eyes met his.

He didn't say anything as he slipped an arm around my naked back and helped me into a sitting position. I realized why he didn't want me to see it, but I felt nothing as I watched the scene play out before me.

Josh was kneeled before Rysten, his mouth gaping open in a now silent scream. The glamor that always surrounded Rysten was nonexistent. A wave of power that smelled distinctly of rot and decay filled the room as he held Josh's face between his hands.

His eyes bled from their sockets as Rysten extracted the only sort of revenge I would ever get to see. I don't think he could have stopped, even if I asked him.

Rysten leaned forward and whispered something in his ear that I couldn't hear. Over his shoulder, Josh's bleeding eyes met mine. Even dying, he looked at me hungrily. I grit my teeth together and said the only thing that could bring me peace.

"Kill him."

My words were a whisper upon his grave. The moment they left my lips, his eyes exploded, and his heart gave out.

I'd never been one to revel in death, but after being stalked, drugged, and defiled, let's just say it does something to your soul. I stared at his corpse, but there was no guilt. No kindness. No remorse.

I wanted him dead because he tried to take from me the very thing that I never wanted to take from anybody: the power to choose.

And if the Horsemen hadn't come, he'd be raping me on a conference room table at this very moment. The truth of that thought hurt more than any physical pain.

But this wasn't the time to process shit.

Not here, in a room where his corpse was still warm, and I was half-naked only being held up by Julian's arm. No. Not here.

Allistair came forward to lift my arms while Julian put my shirt back on me.

I should have worn a bra.

"Listen to me, Ruby," Allistair said. He repeated my name three times before stepping in my field of vision and forcing my attention. "We're going to clean this up. It'll be like it never happened. No one will know where he went, but that human will never hurt you again."

Like it never happened. Those words played over and over in my mind.

"Moira said the same thing," I murmured. Images of a night not so different than this played out before me. About a boy and a girl who played a game, and caught fire.

"What are you talking about?" Allistair asked gently. My thoughts began spinning wildly out of control.

"I never wanted him to lose his mind. I just couldn't stop myself," I whispered.

I could still remember the color of his hair. So yellow; kissed by the sun. He was barely a man when we met.

"Ruby, this isn't your fault. What happened here—"

"He hurt me, too. And I made him pay." My words were so soft. So quiet. Four pairs of eyes turned on me.

"She's in shock, and she's hurting. I'm going to take her home. Get this cleaned up. All of it," Julian commanded. He leaned down and put his other arm beneath my legs. As he carried me out of the conference room, I looked over his shoulder.

Laran held out a hand, and Josh's body went up in flames. Across from him, bathed in the firelight, Rysten's eyes found me. He didn't say anything, but something in the way he watched me made me think he knew what I was talking about. Then again, maybe I was just seeing shadows in the eyes of one killer to another.

No one questioned Julian as he carried me out of Pandora's Box. I had to wonder what kind of security they had here if they just let men carry barely conscious women out the front door. I guess that was humans for you. They were as fucked up and flawed as we demons were. They just turned a blind eye to their own nefariousness.

Outside of the club, the wind picked up and the temperature dropped. I huddled against Julian as he walked farther from the club and turned down an alley. The midnight skies were a welcome sight after what seemed like a trip down the rabbit hole. I breathed a sigh of relief, but it was too soon.

"Going somewhere, mate?"

Glancing over Julian's shoulder, I looked at the entrance to the alleyway behind us.

Devil save us.

It was the imp from the dive-bar, and he brought friends.

CHAPTER 15

"Since when do the Horsemen get involved with human affairs?" the imp called. Wind barreled down the alley and I clung to Julian as he turned towards it. Overhead, a dark cloud covered the moon. Thunder roared as a light drizzle broke out.

"What we do doesn't concern you, imp," Julian sneered. He and Allistair had that cold-arrogance-thing down pat. I didn't feel the need to tremble with Allistair, because he was just condescending towards humans no matter what. Julian was different. There was a chill that followed, like death dancing on the wind.

"Actually," the imp grinned, "it does, since your mate killed half my men and took my eye as a warning." He stepped into the light of the single lamp that hung over a door in the alley.

One eye was glowing red, just as I remembered it. The other was an empty socket, horribly scarred by what looked like knife marks...Laran literally cut his eye out. All for touching me.

On any other day, that thought might make me a bit queasy. Today, I could not bring myself to feel much of anything, except the small bit of self-preservation I still had that wanted to get the fuck away from here.

This was the part where Julian was supposed to say he had nothing to do with it, and let bygones be bygones.

"You touched a she-demon he laid his claim on," Julian replied.

I froze. *What the actual fuck? That's not what you were supposed to say*!

Apparently, the imp thought so as well, because an evil smile that promised very bad things slipped onto his face.

"The very she-demon you're holding now, if memory serves me," the imp commented, his eye dropping from Julian to me. I regarded him warily, wishing no part in this. It was too little, too late.

"She is under our protection. Anyone that thinks to harm her will die a very slow and painful death by my hand. Don't try to cross me, imp. If you thought War's punishment was hard, you will find that Death is much more permanent." Julian's words were brittle. He sounded confident, but I could sense the worry pulsing through him. He may be able to hide it from them, but I knew the truth, and it didn't bode well for me.

"Protection? Your she-demon glamored herself from him and was practically begging to be fucked. I might still oblige when we're finished with you." His gaze roamed over me, far too heated for my liking. "Although, I am curious as to what one single girl could do to provoke the protection of the Four Horsemen. I've been hearing some rumors out of Hell. Interesting rumors. Kind of make a demon wonder..."

Julian bristled against the imp's accusations. He wasn't alone.

"She isn't your concern, though, is she?" Julian asked. I don't know if the imp could tell how hard he was trying to divert their attention, but I sure as hell could. He wasn't panicking by any means, but worry was going head to head with his urge to kill them where they stood.

I was just hoping he would find a way to get us out of here.

"It's because of her your mate did this to me," he said as he pointed at his eye. "I'll think of a suitable punishment when we're done here. If she is who I think she is, my master will be very interested. Perhaps enough to earn me a promotion, after I use her to lure out the other three." I gripped the collar of Julian's jacket to hide my trembling.

The imp whistled as he backed away and the demons in his liege started toward us. Off to the side, one in particular caught my attention.

The bouncer from the club.

I opened my mouth, but before I could say anything, someone lunged. Julian kicked them out of the way and took another one down, but there was no way he was going to win this fight if was holding me.

"Put me down," I said as he dodged a punch.

"Not happening," he grumbled. That was before some of them pulled out knives. He had six demons in front of him, not including one-eye and the pussies that stood watching. Probably trying to make sure I don't escape.

My voice was barely a whisper. "Damn it, Julian. I'm dead weight. I can barely hold onto you. Put me down, or we're both dead." It only took one swipe of a knife and him getting stabbed in the arm for him to listen. Without turning away from our attackers, he swung me behind him.

"Run to the end." I took two steps before dizziness began to overtake me. Damn drugs were still in my system. I managed another two steps before I fell sideways into the wall and collapsed to the ground, dragged down by the heaviness I still couldn't shake.

Dirt smeared my face and hands, and I took a trembling breath. My teeth chattered in the cold and rain. Thank the Devil I couldn't get pneumonia. Then again, maybe a sickness induced death would be kinder than whatever the imp had planned.

Julian was fending quite well for himself, given the bodies that were piling up around him, but there was one problem: the imp had thought ahead and brought scores of demons. For every body that dropped, there was another one waiting to take its place.

Even so, Julian let out an animalistic roar, plunging his hand through a demon's chest, pulling out its still beating heart. My mouth popped open, and in that exact moment, his eyes met mine.

I wish I could say that time stood still, but it was quite the opposite. He had made that one fatal mistake: he took his eyes off the fight.

I saw it coming, but there was nothing I could say to stop it.

A demon wrapped a cord around his neck.

Another gutted him. Again. And again. And again.

Another bashed his knees in with a crow bar.

I watched in horror. I couldn't look away as they surrounded him. They had overpowered him so completely, I couldn't see anything of Julian at all. It was only then that the imp came out of the shadows. He took slow, steady steps toward me. The bouncer from the club fell in line with him.

My heart pounded as I tried to scramble back, stumbling as I searched for false security in the shadows. The imp gave me a lazy smile as he squatted down in front of me.

"Hello, dollface." I glared up at him. "Now, now. No need to be so hateful. We were getting along rather well at our last meeting, before your friends did this." He turned his face so that I was staring into the empty eye socket. "Fortunately for you, I need that face to be pretty in case I'm wrong and my master doesn't want you. Can't sell you off with a missing eye, can I? That's why I have my friend here."

His ink colored hair blew with the wind, water dampening it and causing the ends to stick to his forehead, converging around that terrible scar. He snapped his fingers once, and the bouncer stepped in front of him, blocking my vision. The bouncer glanced back and forth between me and the imp. It didn't take a genius to see he was nervous. Clearly not nervous enough, if he was going along with whatever the red-eyed shit had planned.

"What do you want?" I said in a raspy voice. The imp smiled, and it would have looked genuine, if not for the violent sounds echoing behind him. I didn't dare to look that way, fearing what I might see.

"You can talk. Color me impressed. The drugs he gave the kid should have knocked you out cold," he said.

My heart skipped a beat.

"You gave him that?" I asked, recalling the out-of-body experience. If that's what it did to a demon...that shit would kill a human at its most potent.

"No, I had my mate here do that. He was going to give them to you, but then your boyfriend showed up and had no problem using them himself. Said he didn't care what it took to have you." The imp let out a callous laugh. The scars distorting his once handsome face.

"How'd you even find me?" I breathed in a grated whisper. I just needed to keep them talking until the others arrived. My chances of surviving this night were decreasing with every minute that passed.

"Wasn't that hard, dollface. All my men saw you last Friday in my bar. I gave them all a hefty dose of what was left of my stash after War came through. Told them if they saw you, use it, and call me." Well, that answered that question. At least Moira was safe from all this. Small comfort, as it was.

The ground shook as something let out a terrifying roar. I'd never heard anything so primal or powerful in all my life. Around us, the dead rose up and began attacking the demons still living. It was unlike anything I'd ever seen, but I knew without a doubt who caused it.

"Julian," I whispered.

He was a necromancer. No. He was *the* necromancer. As if the Horsemen of Death wasn't scary enough.

The imp made a motion with his hand, and the bouncer walked forward. Sharp pains pricked the tips of my fingers as I tried to scramble away from him. He reached out and back-handed me across the face.

I didn't even register the pain as my body hit the pavement. My mouth tasted of copper and grit. I turned just in time to see him reach for me again and I spat in his face. Blue blood, mucus and bits of gravel hit his cheek.

"You little bitch," he said. He reached out and tried to grab me, but I planted my foot in his sternum. It was a feeble attempt; my legs had no strength. He let out a growl and threw my leg to the side, pinning me to the asphalt.

Panic ate at me as his hand wrapped around my jaw and squeezed. He reached in his back pocket and pulled out a small baggie. Using his teeth, he ripped the top open and grinned down at me.

"You see these?" he asked me. I didn't dare open my mouth. "I gave your boyfriend two, and you still can't walk. What do you think another two will do?"

I sure as hell wasn't about to find out.

He tightened his grip on my jaw, pressing his fingers in to try to get me to open. I strained against his hold, thrashing as best as I could. He squeezed harder.

The blood in my mouth flowed and the first trickle of pain finally hit me.

Followed by anger.

I scratched and clawed at his arms, but he only

squeezed tighter. My jaw popped, and a sudden, sharp pain filled me. I gasped.

Before I could stop him, he dumped the contents of the baggie straight into my mouth and closed my jaw shut. The pills fizzled within seconds.

It was only a matter of time.

Terror and adrenaline swept through me at the prospect of being taken. My heart pounded harder and faster, and my palms sweat. The rain pelted my face as the thunder roared.

And then the burning started.

A conflagration that couldn't be controlled, a raging inferno tore through my chest. It was icy and hot and electric and grounding all at the same time. It was everything I've ever felt, and nothing at all.

It was a fire so hot, it felt cold.

And somewhere, deep inside me, a door opened.

The beast, my beast, took one look outside of her prison walls, and decided she wasn't going to be confined again.

I screamed against the pain that ripped through me, swallowing the mixture of blood and drugs as I did. The demon that sat on top of me gave me a cruel smile as he moved to hold my arms down. The beast within surged forward, and my screaming came to an abrupt halt. His hands turned black as coal. He jumped away from me, but it was already too late. A devil wearing my face smiled up at him.

CHAPTER 16

"No," he whispered, backing away.

The fire in his veins wouldn't abate. Not until it consumed him.

The darkness spread up his arms, throughout his chest, and to every unseen nook and cranny. I cocked my head to the side as he began clawing at himself. He tore at his clothes, his hair, tearing his very skin in a desperate attempt to escape the fire that took him.

And I felt all of it. His clawing. His tearing. His burning flesh and melting skin.

It was awful. Horrific.

My beast didn't care.

He opened his mouth, maybe to shout or to scream, but no sound came out. It was the kind of pain, so raw, so intense... it was almost unimaginable. He was in his own personal hell and I felt every moment of it as he died.

Pleasure and pain coiled inside of me as I sat back and let the beast have her way.

Blue light shined behind his eyes as the skin around

his face turned black and charred, mirroring the rest of him.

First his hands stopped moving. Then his arms. His legs. When the fire behind his eyes winked out, and all that was left were pits black as sin, I knew he was dead.

A single wind swept down the alleyway, and the husk of the once living bouncer disintegrated into ash. The only hint as to what happened to him was a single blue ember, and then it winked out of existence.

The beast looked to the imp that was backing down the alley. He had thought he could challenge Death, but the sight of me scared him? My beast smiled, and it wasn't kind.

She shifted my body onto its knees, like we were going to make a move for him, and the imp took off running. He bolted like the coward he was, leaving the rest of the men he led here to die. She turned her eyes to the alleyway before us, where the dead bodies that had risen were dropping like flies, their purpose fulfilled now that the once living had joined them in the afterlife.

A hand plunged through the chest of a demon, spraying blood across the already navy tainted cement. The body fell to the ground, and standing there among the chaos, was Julian.

He shook his once blond hair and blue flung from it in droplets. Rain dribbled down his undamaged body. His shirt was torn, exposing lean, unblemished muscle. Blood soaked his pants, his own and theirs. But despite what they'd done in an attempt to kill him, he was perfect. Whole. Only a single cut ran from his brow to his chin, but in the time that we took to stare at one another, that, too, had healed.

Death. He truly was Death.

Could he even be killed?

I wasn't certain, but his flawless unmarked body, free of scars, made me wonder.

"Ruby?" he asked quietly. Hesitant. I wondered what he saw that made him tread so carefully.

"They hurt her." The voice that came out of my mouth was cold. Flat.

Julian nodded his head and held his bloody hands up in surrender. "I know, and I'm sorry I couldn't stop them all sooner. Thank you for taking care of her," he said softly.

The beast didn't respond as he walked towards us. His steps were small; measured and careful. He tread like he was walking on glass. Only when he was standing before us did she speak again.

"They've hurt her before, but I could not save her last time. She does not wish to leave this world, and yet…"—the cold voice trailed off —"if they hurt her again, I will burn it to the ground." There was the softest menace in her voice. The promise of unspeakable horror. A true apocalypse brought forth from our hands. She would make Sodom and Gomorrah look like child's play, brought forth from a benevolent God, because she would wipe the earth clean of all humankind.

It would be the most brutal healing and genocide the earth has ever seen.

And she—*I*—had the power to do it.

Julian didn't flinch. He didn't give any indication that

he was afraid. Feeling his emotions filtering through, there was wariness and some residual pain, but not fear. The beast appreciated that. She could respect that.

Julian crouched on one knee before us, but he made no move to touch. He was smart for that. "I will do better, but right now, I'd like to talk to Ruby." He didn't phrase it as a question. He wasn't asking permission. He was telling her that it was time to recede.

The beast wasn't keen on that idea. She had been locked away for a very long time. So long, she didn't even know who put her in her prison.

"How do I know that I will not be caged again?" she asked. It wasn't child-like or inquisitive. The voice was lifeless, but there was an icy undercurrent that held a rage of its own. Julian stared at us for a long moment and spoke with absolute authority.

"Because I will kill any who try."

The beast liked that. She liked that very much.

I reached out to coax her back, and this time she agreed to recede, knowing that she would not be imprisoned again.

"Take care of her." Her parting words.

An invisible force shoved me into my own body again. A whimpered moan escaped my lips as the weariness of the night weighed on me. The gravel that pricked at my knees hurt, sharper than it should. The dizziness in my head was all too familiar after the first time being drugged. My consciousness was already beginning to wane.

"Ruby," Julian said as he breathed a sigh of relief. "Are you okay?"

"Force...drugs...want...h-home," I slurred. The effects were already coming back. I probably had moments before the paralysis and out-of-body experience returned, but this time, I wouldn't be alone. The beast was there, waiting through it with me.

Julian didn't hesitate as he picked me up and strolled down the alley. I looked over his shoulder at the scene behind us. Dead bodies lay in heaps on the alley floor. Their arms and legs were bent at odd angles. Some had gaping holes in their chest cavities, others were decapitated.

Julian truly was a monster.

But then again, maybe I was, too.

Ashes blowing in the wind, the last thing I saw before we stepped into the shadows and it all went black.

The endless darkness only lasted a second before he was carrying me through my front yard. He can shadow walk. Now I knew how they got around so easily. The thought was only of passing interest when I realized Moira's car wasn't there.

The driveway was dark, but Julian navigated just fine as he ascended the porch. "Where's your spare key?" he asked. My head lolled against his shoulder.

"Don't...one," I mumbled. He didn't say anything, didn't sigh in annoyance. He simply moved to hold me with one arm. There was a sharp crunching sound, that I assumed was him breaking the lock, and then the door opened.

The blood curdling screech that awaited us stirred me from the drugged-out haze settling in. Julian let out a curse as something flew at him full force before settling on my chest. We weren't even through the doorway completely, but Bandit was here and waiting.

"Hey...bub-by," I slurred. My raccoon wrapped his arms around my neck and purred louder than I'd ever heard him. Maybe that was just the drugs.

Julian kicked the door shut behind him and flipped the light on as he moved into the house. My living room disappeared as he rounded the corner to my room. He laid me down in bed, pulling the covers around me. I was already far enough gone that my arms and legs were useless, and the feeling of helplessness crept in. The beast inside me twitched, pacing uneasily. She didn't like this anymore than I did, but sometimes there was truly nothing you could do except wait it out.

"What can I do?" Julian asked, his voice tense. Strained.

"Lights," I murmured. Bandit snuggled closer to my chest, and right then it was the only thing that kept me sane. That kept the panic at bay.

"What else? What do you need? How do I fix this?" he asked. I could hear the desperation in his voice, but his emotions were lost on me. I couldn't feel them. I couldn't feel much of anything, except the contentment coming from Bandit.

"Can't..." I croaked. "M-m-moira. W-w-wa-want Mmm—" I strained against the pressing weight sitting on my chest, but I hoped he got the message. Eyes heavy and fluttering, I stared at the ceiling. I started to drift across the universe. Time itself was transcended as the violet and blue lights of the club swirled around me again.

I became lost in a world of memories and nightmares.

People's faces, men's faces, passed me by as I waded through. Then came Josh, and the imp, and the bouncer, and Danny...as they all bled together into one. I saw the faces of times gone by, and they slipped through my fingers like smoke, always eluding me.

But then the faces changed. And the lights grew bright. And when the smoked settled, all that remained was fire. The flames were black and shades of blue as they danced through my dreams.

They were the flames I've dreamed of ever since I was a little girl. They were the flames of Hell. The only thing in this world that could outright kill a demon—outside of Death himself. I suppose that should be strange, but I was a demon dreaming of things that little demon girls do. Flames and fire and ash. They gave off no smoke, but they destroyed everything they touched.

It was within those flames that a beast led me, hand-in-hand, to a new place.

Where the pain couldn't reach me, and the demons couldn't find me, and people on earth could no longer hurt me.

Because I was one with the flame.

One with the fire that burned inside my soul.

JULIAN

I didn't know how to help her. I didn't know what to say that could make this better, or make up for the pain that I couldn't save her from. The human drugged her with black lotus, and then molested her. He would have raped her, had she not called out. It was the hurt she projected in a cry for help that led us there. That let us save her. I don't think she even realized she had done it. But if Ruby was as strong as I think she was...we weren't the only ones that felt it.

If my instincts proved right, demons would be coming for her from all corners of the earth. Some would want favor. Some would seek to control her. Others would simply wish to kill her in a bid to open the gates of Hell.

I thought we had more time. I'd hoped we could get to know her better. I'd wanted her to come to it on her own, but time was running out. Even if her psychic assault didn't reach another soul past the four of us, we had a bigger problem.

The beast had awoken, and with it would come the transition. Maybe not tonight, or tomorrow, or even next week, but it would come. And we needed to be ready when it did.

Lucifer had created us to be able to handle the beast. To ground her when she could not ground herself. If we were to have any hope of being able to do that, we needed her to trust us.

Trust isn't earned lightly, and it takes time. More time than we had. If she really was on the verge of the transition, we didn't have more than a month. And that was a generous estimate.

The front door flew open, and a tiny green-haired banshee stormed around the corner. The girl didn't even look to me, her eyes frantic as they sought a single person. I moved aside for her, hoping she could do what I and the others could not.

She ripped off her heels fiercely and climbed into bed next to Ruby. Her slender green arms wrapped around Ruby's slightly wider shoulders. She began murmuring things under her breath, but I closed the door. The things said between two people that close were not meant for others to hear. Certainly not after a night like tonight.

I walked back down the hall and into the living room where the other three waited. Rysten was seated on the couch, staring with a vacantness that was telling. Allistair faced the window, his back to us and his posture stiff. Unyielding. Laran paced before the door and the wind blew harder outside. The moon had been eclipsed by dark clouds as heavy rain came down. The forecast hadn't called for rain this night, which meant it was War.

"Is it taken care of?" I asked.

Laran nodded. "The bodies have been burned; the ashes scattered. No one will know what happened. They never existed as far as this world is concerned." He was the most solemn I'd seen him since the Ring Wars.

"And the human?" I asked. If I didn't have Ruby's needs to be concerned with, I'd be calling him back from the veil right this moment to make him pay ten times over. Twenty. I could make him relive his death a hundred times.

But it would never be enough for what he did to her, and she didn't need to know *that* particular aspect of my power just yet.

"I've erased every trace of him online. Social media. Bank accounts. Vendor accounts. Birth certificate. Social security. It's gone. All of it. But unless any of us suddenly learned how to take people's memories...it will be impossible to erase his memory from her life completely." Rysten blew out a harsh breath. "Humans will remember him, but there is no evidence that his disappearance could be linked to her."

I nodded once, but it was Famine that spoke. "That's the best we can hope for, unless we plan to kill everyone he ever knew." I considered the validity of that statement. Weighing the good and the bad, the domino effect that would have.

"The imp with one eye escaped. We need to prioritize hunting him down before he becomes a problem," I replied. Laran nodded, but he wasn't as enthusiastic as he usually was about the prospect of hunting. I couldn't blame him; not when failure sat like a stone upon our backs.

"There's more...say it" Rysten prompted. I turned to my brother. The darkness I knew well still hadn't left his eyes. Killing the human wasn't enough. Many were going to die tonight when this conversation was over.

"The beast has awoken. One of the demons got to her, and she burned him alive from the inside out," I replied. Rysten nodded. He must have sensed it the same as I had.

"She's stronger than she realizes. I don't know how she's repressed her powers this long, but I don't think it's a coincidence she hasn't gone through the transition yet. Something happened to her, and I'm not talking about tonight," Rysten said.

Silence spread between the four of us, the air thick with things unsaid.

We saved our apologies, our hurt, our sorrows, because they were not meant for each other. It was not each other we failed, but Ruby. If Rysten was right, it was possible we failed long before we even came for her.

If something happened in her past to cause her to suppress the transition, it was enough to make me question if we were right sending her to this world in the first place.

To a world where monsters and men were the same thing.

CHAPTER 17

I WOKE UP TOASTY WARM, AND PANIC IMMEDIATELY replaced the calm a deep sleep had given me. My eyes flew open, expecting flames and a burning house, but no such sight awaited me.

My room was dimly lit, cast in a warm yellow glow. On one side of me, Bandit was sprawled on his back, his head pillowed by my arm that he had drooled all over. On the other side was Moira, still wearing her dress from the night before. Her arm was slung across my bare waist, wrapped protectively around me.

Then the memories from last night came flooding back.

The club. The drugs. Josh. The imp. The bouncer. The fire.

My beast.

I didn't even need to check that it was true, because she was still there. Right in the back of my mind, watching me and waiting for the moment she was needed.

I swallowed hard, and my throat protested loudly. It was as parched as the desert. I moved to shimmy out from beneath Moira and Bandit, but she tightened her hold on me, and my best friend looked up.

All it took was one look from her and tears formed in the corners of my eyes.

"Oh, honey..." she whispered and held me tighter.

"How much do you know?" I rasped.

"Not much. Allistair came and found me last night. Told me some bad shit went down and you were drugged," she murmured against my shoulder.

"Did he really say that?" I asked.

"That some bad shit went down?" she asked. I nodded. "No. I'm paraphrasing. He used more adulty words, but I kind of lost my shit because I knew something was up before he found me. You didn't come back. I was looking everywhere for you. They brought me home and I saw you lying in bed—" She stopped and hugged me tighter.

"I killed someone, Moira," I whispered.

She didn't even hesitate. "They probably deserved it."

I choked back the sob that threatened to escape me. Whether from shock or gratitude, I didn't know. What I did know was that Moira was the best fucking friend that I could ever ask for.

"You don't have to talk about it. Just tell me where, and I can bury the body. No one will ever know." Wet tears streamed down my face as I hugged her tighter. The dryness in my throat stung as I tried to swallow the lump that formed.

Devil knows what I did to deserve her.

"He's already gone," I whispered.

"What do you mean?"

I took a deep breath. I was prepared to tell her everything, but not yet.

"Can I take a shower first? I feel disgusting, and after —" I didn't even have to finish. Moira unwound herself from me and jumped out of bed. Her makeup smeared across her face, and black tear marks trailed from her eyes to her chin.

"You don't have to explain yourself. I'm going to go start some tea and make a pot of coffee. I'll be in the living room when you're done." She smiled weakly and left me to my own devices. I was probably supposed to cry then. It would have made sense.

Cry for myself. Cry because I killed someone. Hell. Maybe if I were another girl, I would have cried for the man I killed.

They were rapists and killers, and I wouldn't cry for that.

They didn't deserve my tears.

I inhaled through my nose and gently removed my arm from underneath Bandit. He rolled over onto my pillow and left a trail of slobber behind. At least some things never change.

The transition from laying down to standing was harder. My head began pounding, and the room swayed. I took it slow, gripping the headboard as I went. When my feet touched the floor, it took a minute to adjust before standing. Oddly enough, the shift to standing wasn't terrible. My legs felt weak, wobbly. I suppose that getting drugged twice in one night will do that to you.

I made a promise to myself right there: no more bars. Me and Moira could get drunk at home if we wanted, but I wasn't stepping foot in another fucking bar as long as I lived.

My first steps towards the bathroom were slow and shaky, but they were steadier by the time I reached the door. I gripped the handle tightly, ignoring the mirror as I entered. I didn't want to see myself like this. That might actually break me.

I crossed the cool tile floors, staring at my feet as I went. My mind was numb. My body acted without thought. The throbbing in my throat stung, but the grime against my skin was worse. I was dirty in a way that even water couldn't clean, but that wouldn't stop me from trying.

My skin reeked of sweat and alcohol.

I stepped into the shower, still clothed, and flipped it on. Even the memory of where Josh's fingers and mouth had been made me want to scream. Not in pain, but in fury.

I tore at the shirt plastered to my chest, shredding the fabric until it no longer clung to my skin, littering the floor of my shower in scraps and pieces. The rest of my clothes followed. I would burn what was left of them before the day was over.

I scrubbed the shampoo into my hair, washing away the sweat, dirt, and ash that coated me. I emptied the body wash onto myself as I tried to scratch my skin clean with the loofah.

My hair smelled of lavender, and my skin was red and raw, but it wasn't clean enough. Inside me, the beast paced. She didn't like this. She thought it was pointless. She'd rather be out there burning the world down. I ignored her as I let out the one and only scream I would allow myself.

After this, what's done is done. I would give myself these few minutes. Not to cry. Not to anguish over the demons that died, or my would-have-been rapist.

I screamed because I could.

Because it happened.

Because I was violated.

Because words could not describe what I felt, but the animalistic roar was as close as I could get.

When my voice broke and my ears rang, the back of my throat raw and tasting of blood, I finally heaved a sigh of relief and let go of the sponge. I turned the water off and stepped out of the shower, feeling lighter than before. I dried my skin with a clean towel and wrapped it around my waist. While brushing my teeth, something caught my eye in the mirror and the toothbrush fell from my fingers.

Five points now adorned my sternum. Black lines connected them. A circle ran around the edges. And the realization of what I was staring at made the beast within me purr.

After twenty-three years of believing I was half-demon, an upside-down pentagram formed between my breasts.

I had a brand. Which meant I would transition.

That brand was Lucifer's mark.

I tore my eyes away from the mark on my chest and brushed my teeth as quickly as possible. I didn't want to look at it. Not today. Today, I would be Ruby. Just Ruby. The tattoo artist who had a pet raccoon and a crazy best friend.

Today, I would eat a bucket of Rocky Road ice cream. I would drink two pots of Earl Grey, and spend the entire day laying on my sofa watching Viola Davis and her team of wannabe lawyers. I would wear pajamas and make Moira braid my hair because I was too lazy to do it.

Today, I was the half-succubus from Portland, who attracted more trouble than even the Horsemen of Hell knew what to do with.

Tomorrow, I would be Lucifer's daughter.

The demon destined to be the next ruler of Hell.

But today, I was just Ruby.

To be continued...

IF YOU LOVED this book and want to connect more with Kel and her other readers, please join her Facebook Readers Group at https://www.facebook.com/groups/kelskrew/ for more shenanigans!

ABOUT THE AUTHOR

Kel Carpenter is a master of werdz. When she's not reading or writing, she's traveling the world, lovingly pestering her editor, and spending time with her husband and fur-babies. She is always on the search for good tacos and the best pizza. She resides in Bethesda, MD and desperately tries to avoid the traffic.

Join Kel's Readers Group!

ACKNOWLEDGMENTS

This story started as one thing, and grew well beyond what I had intended. I have my tribe to thank for that. Analisa and Carrie are not only my shitty coworkers that bitch with me, and probably about me, but they also are like family in that they've stood beside me despite my bad days (and there are plenty of them). My boyfriend can attest to that. Matt has been wonderful throughout my journey as an author. He's good at remembering to feed me and take me on walks, even when I forget to do so myself. Perhaps the most important person of all though, is my coffee gopher. Not only does she bring me coffee, but she would kill me if she was not mentioned here. So, thank you, Courtney, for listening to all my caffeine withdrawal induced ramblings and being the first person to always read biographies I record for the voices.

And finally, to my readers, thank you for buying my books and enabling my coffee addiction. It means the world to me.

NOVEMBER SCAVENGER HUNT

The word for this book is:
Dingleberry

Lightning Source UK Ltd.
Milton Keynes UK
UKHW010941060121
376524UK00001B/74